"Did you have dishonorable intentions?"

She wondered what he'd thought when he'd come downstairs last night while she was asleep.

"Let's just say it was good that you were asleep," Quinn murmured with no humor.

"What if I hadn't been?" Would she have been playing with fire the way she sensed she was at this moment?

He leveled those silver eyes on her. "If you hadn't been, I'd've done something I'd probably be regretting right now." He took a deep breath and glared at her. "Look, we don't even know who you are—if you're married, if you're madly in love with someone. Now, I don't know how you read that, but to me it means hands-off." Each of the words was spoken with deliberate intensity through clenched teeth.

And as she watched him storm out of the room, she couldn't suppress the guilty wish that she'd been awake when he'd come down last night.

Dear Reader,

Welcome to Strummel Investigations, where a typical day is anything but dull. This family of top-notch investigators pursues the most baffling cases...and gets intimately involved with their clients!

We're so pleased—and we know you'll be, too—to welcome Victoria Pade to American Romance. This prolific and bestselling writer makes her debut in the series with the lighthearted, fun Strummel Investigations trilogy.

Getting to know Quinn, Lindsey and Logan is a great way to spend your summer! Be sure to look for all the Strummel Investigations titles.

Regards,

Debra Matteucci
Senior Editor & Editorial Coordinator
Harlequin Books
300 East 42nd Street, 6th Floor
New York, NY 10017

Victoria Pade

THE CASE OF THE BORROWED BRIDE

Harlequin Books

TORONTO • NEW YORK • LONDON
AMSTERDAM • PARIS • SYDNEY • HAMBURG
STOCKHOLM • ATHENS • TOKYO • MILAN
MADRID • WARSAW • BUDAPEST • AUCKLAND

ISBN 0-373-16588-9

THE CASE OF THE BORROWED BRIDE

Chapter One

She knew her name was Cara.

Well, she didn't know it with any real certainty. What she knew was that when she'd found a bush behind which to answer the call of nature and hiked up the full skirt of the wedding dress she was wearing, she'd discovered a garter with Cara and Peter embroidered on it.

She assumed she wasn't Peter.

The only other thing she knew was that within the past few minutes she'd awakened lying in what appeared to be a mountain meadow. *A secluded mountain meadow,* she thought as she glanced around at the wildflowers that grew like a lush carpet amid aspen trees and moss-covered rocks, below the steep slopes of fir-covered peaks all around.

Not a single man-made sound drifted to her, not even from far away, and the road that ran along the edge of the field was nothing more than two wheel ruts in the dirt.

But worse than the sense that she was a long way from civilization, when she tried to figure out where she might be, she realized that she didn't even have the foggiest idea what city she might be in. Or what state.

Or even what country. Because there was only a great big fuzzy blank where her memory should have been— somewhere behind the blinding headache that emanated from the lump on the right side of her head, which also accounted for the profuse amount of blood that stained the bodice of her lacy gown.

A sudden wave of dizziness sat her back on the ground where she'd been standing looking around to get her bearings. She closed her eyes against the accompanying surge of pain through her head and then opened them again, back to the brightness of what looked to be the last of the day's sunshine.

"Come on, you must know who you are," she said out loud to herself. But even the sound of her own voice seemed unfamiliar to her.

And no matter how hard she tried to recall something—anything—she couldn't.

She honestly didn't know who she was. Or where she'd come from. Or how she'd gotten there. Or how old she was. Or who her family or friends were. Or what she did for a living. Or her phone number.

Nothing.

She didn't remember a single thing.

"Well," she said on a forlorn sigh.

But the fact that the sun was very near to disappearing behind one of the surrounding mountains, and would before long leave her in the dark, made it seem less important to sit there and try to force something that wouldn't come than to see what she could do about getting herself out of there.

She got to her feet again, discovering her knees weren't any less wobbly than they'd been on her trek to the bush and back. For a moment she just stood there to gain her balance. Then, with an off-kilter equilibrium, she headed for the road.

It didn't help that the heel of one of her soiled satin pumps was missing, and she thought that if anyone saw her they'd no doubt believe she was drunk.

At that moment it would have been worth it just to have some assistance because each step rippled into an aftershock in her brain, sapping her strength and energy.

She barely made it to the road before she had to stop and sit down again, this time leaning against a rock.

Her head was spinning and throbbing and sickeningly light, and she was as exhausted as if she'd just walked ten miles instead of ten feet.

"Cara Whatever-your-name-is, you are in quite a pickle here," she said out loud again as she wondered how she was going to get anywhere feeling the way she did.

Her view from this spot wasn't any more encouraging or enlightening than it had been from the middle of the meadow. There were still no signs of life. And that sun seemed to sink lower every time she looked at it. She was going to have to try to go on and that was all there was to it.

"Where are those knights on white chargers when you need them?"

She looked for an indication of which way to go when she stored up a little more stamina, but there didn't seem to be one. The road didn't rise or fall. It didn't reveal anything at either end but more road.

What if she chose the wrong way and headed farther into the mountains and away from any kind of help?

"Oh, that's smart, Cara Whatever-your-name-is. Panic. That'll do a lot of good."

No, she decided, she couldn't think about getting herself into worse shape by going the wrong direction. Surely the road had to lead from somewhere to somewhere else, so either way she'd come upon something.

She laid her head against the rock and closed her eyes once more.

Just a little rest and then she'd go on. She'd find a house with a telephone. Or a main road with a policeman. Or a nice passerby who would pick her up.

She'd be fine, she reassured herself, drifting toward an overwhelming need to sleep.

That was when she heard the first faint sound of a car.

Her eyes flew open and she sat up, listening, hoping she hadn't just dozed off and dreamed it.

But she hadn't. She could definitely hear a car engine.

Please let it be coming down this road.

She used the rock as a brace as she got to her feet again, leaning her hips against it for support once she was standing so she could flag down the driver when the car passed.

If it passed.

It did, at a speed too fast to accommodate the weather-beaten, bumpy road. It wasn't a knight on a white charger, it was a man in a white sports coupe.

"No problem, a car is better than a horse, anyway," she said, as if someone had been listening to her request and granted it.

The driver did a double take when he saw her and slammed on his brakes, coming to a stop several dozen feet in front of her.

After a moment of staring at her from the car as if he couldn't believe what he was seeing, he opened his door. What looked to be about six feet three inches of solid, packed muscle unfolded from behind the wheel to stare at her over the roof.

Did she know him? she wondered. After all, she didn't remember her own name. He could be her brother or her groom for all she knew.

Or he could be someone she didn't know and wouldn't want to—

It suddenly occurred to her just how vulnerable she was. But he had pearl gray eyes that looked nice—in a surprised sort of way. So she swallowed, tried not to think of serial killers and gave a weak little wave that no doubt looked silly under the circumstances.

But then, what was the proper protocol for circumstances like these?

He didn't wave back. He didn't answer her feeble smile with one of his own. He merely stared at her and said, "What the hell?" in a voice that could have been very intimidating if he'd let it.

"I'm in sort of a mess." Ah, that was who she was— Cara, Queen of Understatement.

The man reached into the car's interior and turned off his engine. He left his door open and rounded the front end.

Cara pressed back against the rock, wanting to put it between her and the stranger but also not wishing to offend her rescuer. Or at least who she hoped to be her rescuer.

He seemed to sense her uneasiness, because he stopped several nonthreatening feet from her. "Are you okay?" That sounded better than "What the hell?"

"Well, not completely okay, no."

He nodded. "Stupid question. Obviously you're not okay." He took his wallet out of the back pocket of the tight jeans he wore and handed her a driver's license and a business card from it by just leaning forward. "Here, don't be afraid. Let's start over. My name is Quinn Strummel."

Still leaning against the rock, Cara reached out to take what he offered. It was a good sign, she decided. He wouldn't have introduced himself and presented identification if he meant her any harm, would he?

But as she tried to read, she realized her vision was blurred. Whether from the bump on the head or because she was naturally farsighted, she couldn't say, but she couldn't see any of the small print and she could barely make out Strummel Investigations in large block letters in the center of the card.

Private investigations? The man was a detective? That seemed nearly as good as a policeman and it helped her relax slightly as she handed the card and the driver's license back to him.

"Are you...investigating something?"

He laughed wryly, a rich, easy sound. "I have a cabin up this road about five miles. I've been there for the last couple of days. I was just headed back to the city."

She motioned toward the meadow. "Is this your property, too?"

"Yes, as a matter of fact, it is."

"Then I guess I'm trespassing."

"Technically I guess you are."

She was also buying herself some time to study him. He was as solid as a boxer, with shoulders a mile wide and biceps that stretched the short sleeves of his white polo shirt almost to the breaking point. His waist was narrow, and his legs were long, hard and powerful, if the way they strained the denim of his jeans was any indication.

His face was an odd but very attractive combination, both rugged and studious looking. He had a serious brow beneath hair the color of Russian mink, which fell onto his forehead a little rakishly. His nose was sleek and slightly long, and a pronounced bone structure made deeply indented planes of his cheeks and gave him a sharp jawline and a strong chin, while his mouth was pale and just full enough to suit him.

"And your name is?" he prompted then.

"Oh." Jolted from her reverie, she didn't think about what she was doing before lifting her skirt high enough to exhibit the garter just above her knee, pointing to it as if it were her version of ID. "I guess it's Cara." But then she realized it probably wasn't a good idea to flash even a little leg at a complete stranger— private investigator or not—and dropped her hem in a hurry. It unnerved her all over again that his gaze was slow in rising.

When it finally reached her eyes, he frowned. "You *guess* your name is Cara?"

Trying not to sound like a total idiot, she explained both her recent awakening and her completely blank memory.

"Would you mind if I take a look at your head wound?" he asked when she'd finished. He won points for not responding as if she were a nutcase, which she wasn't completely sure of herself, but still the idea of this large stranger getting close enough to touch her made her feel vulnerable all over again.

Her uneasiness must have showed because he said, "I won't hurt you." Then, as if he'd thought of something else, he went back to his car, took a baseball bat from his back seat and brought it to her, keeping his distance to hold it out to her in the same way he had with his license and card before. "Here, if it'll make you feel better you can hang on to this for protection."

She took it but she didn't feel a whole lot better. The man was clearly as strong as an ox. He could take the bat away from her without much trouble, and she knew it. But she raised her chin as if she were tough as nails and said okay to his request to look at the lump on her head.

One step closed the gap between them. "I'm going to need to move your hair out of the way," he said as if she were a skittish colt, before raising his hands to do it.

Big hands, she noticed, with long, masculine fingers that could be surprisingly gentle as he moved aside her matted hair.

Standing as near as he was, she also became aware of a light, clean scent of after-shave. It made her consider, for the first time, her own hygiene. She was covered in dried blood, and doubted if being unconscious for any amount of time gave a person good breath.

She tried not to breathe at all while he was so close, wondering, too, how awful she looked. That was when she realized she didn't even have a mental image of her own face. Could be she had a big, bent nose, and crossed, bloodshot eyes, and eyebrows like overgrown bushes, and stained teeth, and blotchy skin, and elephant ears. And jowls, too. Hanging down, wobbly jowls...

Oh, she hoped not!

This man was very attractive. More attractive than her blurry vision had let her know until he'd moved nearer. And here she was a bloody, probably smelly, mess. She hoped she was at least not Cara the Ugly Woman, to boot.

And then she silently reprimanded herself for the silly thought. This wasn't a blind date, for crying out loud.

When his examination of her head was finished he stepped back, though not as far as he'd been before. "I'd say you've been shot."

"Shot?" That made her forget how she looked. "You mean with a gun?"

"I don't think a peashooter would have done it. Looks to me like a bullet fired from behind grazed you." He walked around her then, assessing the rest of her and giving her a list of what he found along the way. "One of your sleeves is torn at the front of the seam. The back of your skirt looks as if it's been slopped through mud." He raised the hem just to her ankles, then dropped it and came back to face her. "And your shoes are scuffed up the backs. I'd say somebody shot you, dragged you and dumped you here in Cold Creek Canyon, Colorado, on your wedding day. But figuring out that last one is too easy to take credit for."

"Oh, that can't be," she said as firmly as if she had something to base her rebuttal on.

"What can't be?"

"Any of it. I mean, I'll grant you that I can't even remember my name, let alone what happened, but I feel like a pretty regular person and pretty regular people don't get shot on their wedding day, dragged to a canyon and dumped."

He studied her as if allowing her doubts. But a corner of his mouth quirked up as if he were fighting a smile at her response. "How exactly does it feel to be *not* a pretty regular person?"

"Well, I just don't feel . . . I don't know . . . like someone who would be shot."

He nodded slowly while he suppressed a full smile. "What do you think happened?"

Her head hurt too much to think at all but she gave it a try, anyway. "How about prewedding jitters?" She glanced at her hands and then held them up as if they supported her theory. "No rings! Maybe at the last minute I just ran away." She demonstrated with a flourish of those ringless hands before needing to pat down the profusion of ruffles that kept creeping up to her chin from the gown's neckline.

"Whoever dumped you here could have stolen your rings," he countered. "No rings doesn't necessarily mean you didn't go through with the wedding."

She didn't feel married, either, but knew he wouldn't take that to mean anything. Nor should she, she told herself.

"So you think you got nervous and ran away from your wedding," he repeated. Then he glanced around. "And how did you get here?"

"The wedding was nearby?" she guessed, as if he could tell her if she were right or wrong.

He shook his head. "No church or chapel for miles."

"It could have been an outdoor ceremony."

"True. But I've been hiking all over these hills for two days and haven't seen anything going on any place that would be a likely site for a wedding. And even then you would have needed to get from there to here some way."

"Well, I must have driven," she reasoned. "That's it. I must have driven off from the wedding and lost my way. And maybe I got out of the car for some reason—" she was thinking about that earlier call of nature but didn't want to say it "—and my heel broke and I fell and bumped my head on a rock."

This time he looked up and down the road. "So where's your car?"

She knew this supposition was getting more and more farfetched, but anything seemed likelier than someone shooting her. "Stolen? Or towed? Maybe the police came by, saw it and thought it was abandoned."

"Without looking around and finding you? Sorry, that one doesn't fly at all. I was a cop. My father was a cop. My brother still is a cop. Cops would have searched for a driver. Besides, this is a private road that goes from the main highway straight up to my cabin where it stops. The police don't patrol it and car thieves aren't likely to have happened by."

She was dizzy again and feeling very punk and weak-kneed. She was afraid if she didn't sit down she was going to faint, so she slid to the ground, using the baseball bat for a crutch and leaning back against the rock. "Okay, so there are a few holes in the theory. I just can't believe someone shot me, of all things."

He hunkered down on his heels so he was level with her and examined her eyes from beneath a sudden frown. "I'm sorry. This isn't the time to postulate. Are you going to pass out on me?"

"I don't think so. Not if I sit a minute."

"I also should have asked, are you hurt anywhere besides your head? Do you feel as if something more was done to you?"

His tone was ominous and she knew what he meant. "No, I haven't been assaulted or anything. I really think I just fell and bumped my head."

He stayed where he was, watching her so intently it became unnerving. She began to think she could actually feel heat coming from those sparkling silver eyes of his.

A trick of her head injury, she told herself, though that didn't explain why she should be noticing how lovely his eyes were.

"Are you looking for clues?" she asked him deadpan so he'd stop staring at her and giving her those hot flashes.

It made him smile that one-sided smile again. "I was just trying to see if you're all right. Why don't you point out where you were when you came to. I can look for clues there while you rest."

She pointed to the spot, though he'd have been able to find it himself—it was the only concentration of squashed wildflowers and meadow grass.

He went to it and did a slow walk around the area, studying every inch before moving on, clearly knowing what he was doing as he widened his circle and somehow even found a trail of broken stems to indicate her path from the road.

And while he was at it, she watched him. He seemed very capable, she realized. And, in spite of his size, gentle, too. He'd been compassionate and considerate, as well as conscientious. He could have just had her get in the car, taken her to the nearest rest stop and let her off. Instead he showed concern for her health, had tried to ease her fears of him and was even searching for anything that might be a piece of this puzzle she'd awakened to.

It all served to convince her that she didn't have anything to fear from him, stranger or not.

When he'd searched the rest of the meadow, too, he came back to her, carrying the single thing he'd found. "The heel to your shoe," he said, holding it up for her to see. "Scraped up the back and cracked from there, too."

She knew he considered that further support of his theory but she still didn't believe it. She'd have told him so except that she was seriously wilting in spite of the fact that she was sitting down.

He hunkered to his heels again, bracing his elbows on his knees and letting his hands dangle between the spread of massive thighs as he once more scanned her face.

"We need to get you to a hospital. While they clean you up and check you over I'll call my brother to see if there's a missing-persons report on you. Could be we'll have you tucked into your own bed by tonight."

The words were meant to comfort her, said in a deep bass voice that sounded so calm and confident and soothing that it invited her to give herself over to his care. Cara wasn't sure she believed they'd be able to get her fixed up and back home that easily when she didn't know where home was, but it was nice to hear, anyway. It said the man had a plan. It said he was going to help her. And right then she needed that.

"Let's get you to the car," he suggested, holding out his hand to her.

She took it and used the baseball bat, too, to get to her feet again. But once she was there she swayed and would have fallen if not for his wrapping a quick arm around her waist to catch her.

"Wobbly knees," she informed him.

Without asking, he scooped her up into his arms the way her groom might have carried her across the threshold.

"Oh, no, I'll get gunk on you," she protested, but no sooner were the words out than he'd taken her to the sports coupe, set her in the passenger seat and belted her in all safe and sound, the baseball bat across her lap.

Then he went around and slipped into the driver's side.

As he fastened his own seat belt and started the engine, she glanced over at him and smiled, though she could feel how weak it was. "I really appreciate your help."

"Don't mention it. I've always been a sucker for damsels in distress," he told her wryly.

"That makes sense since just before you showed up I'd wished for a knight on a white charger."

"I hope a P.I. in a sports car wasn't a disappointment."

"Well, no. You'll do in a pinch. I'm probably allergic to horsehair anyway."

"I understand that's the main problem knights on white chargers have."

"But just for the heck of it, tell me you aren't in the white-slavery trade," she said, mostly joking now.

"White slavery?"

"A person can't be too cautious, you know."

"You are a very strange lady, do you know that? I've never come across someone in trouble who makes wisecracks about it."

"But just for the heck of it, tell me you aren't in the white-slavery trade, anyway."

"I am not in the white-slavery trade," he parroted, as his nice mouth eased into a grin.

"Any other dastardly deeds in your history?" she asked weakly, giving in to the need to lay her head against the headrest, which then required her to blow a flounce of lace from in front of her face.

"I took a lollipop out of a man's pocket at the circus when I was eight. But I was severely reprimanded."

"No problem. This wedding gown has enough ruffles to suffocate me but it's fresh out of pockets." She closed her eyes against a sudden pain that shot through her brain and when she opened them again he wasn't smiling anymore. Instead he looked very solemnly into her eyes and covered one of her hands with his.

"Why don't you just rest? We'll sort through this whole thing when we get to Denver."

"Okay. Then get this white charger in gear and let's go," she said, closing her eyes yet again and trying not to notice the delicious—if inappropriate—waves of warmth that ran right up her arm when he squeezed her hand just before letting it go.

Chapter Two

The emergency room waiting area was painted a dusky yellow color. Brown vinyl chairs lined the walls, separated at the corners by Formica-covered end tables littered with magazines.

After four hours there, Quinn had discovered where a child had carved the name Ashley in the wall behind the small play table, counted the chairs and read nearly every magazine, along with sitting through the wailing of a little boy who looked to have broken his finger and the arrival and departure of a number of other injured and ailing people. And all he knew about Cara was what he could glean from the desk nurse—she was having a battery of tests but she did not need to be admitted and would be released when the tests were completed. Which could be any minute or another four hours.

He hated hospitals.

He stretched his legs out, crossed them at the ankles, rested his head back against the wall and asked himself what the hell he was still doing there.

Curiosity?

Sure. He couldn't help wondering who Cara was, where she came from, what had happened to her. And without a shred of identification or memory, she was in trouble even without factoring in that someone had most likely shot her and left her in that meadow, probably to die.

So he felt a sense of responsibility, he realized at the end of that train of thought. Well, that was misplaced. Rescuing her didn't mean he was taking on her or her problems. After all, she hadn't hired him. He'd just done what anyone might have by picking her up and bringing her to the hospital.

Except that here he was, and not just anyone who picked her up would be dumb enough to still be hanging around, a niggling voice in the back of his mind taunted.

Oh, hell, what was he going to do? Just drop her off and never know what happened to her?

He couldn't do that. It would drive him crazy. It was what had driven him crazy as a cop—that open end. If he were still a cop he would have picked her up, brought her to the hospital and that would have been that for him. What happened to her from there would have been out of his hands and into those of someone in missing persons and someone else from social services.

And too often when things left his hands they got screwed up. Sometimes with devastating results.

So here he was. For the last four hours and God only knew how much longer.

Maybe he'd take a nap.

He closed his eyes and a sudden, vivid image came into mental view—his first sight of Cara. Leaning on that rock, small, fragile looking, her incredible violet eyes wide and hopeful and slightly dazed. Even dressed in that ruined wedding gown, her hair matted with blood, he could tell she was beautiful. A porcelain doll someone hadn't taken care not to harm.

But she was a porcelain doll with spunk, and that thought made him smile.

He liked her fire, that special something that caused her to treat her unusual situation with a wry humor when someone else might have been hysterical.

Great legs, too, although he certainly hadn't expected her to raise her skirt to show him her garter as identification. It had taken him off guard, and despite years of training to be impartial and nonreactionary, his instant response had been as a man. He'd appreciated the sight.

Very unprofessional. For a cop or a P.I. Unprofessional enough to make him uneasy. And not just because he'd liked her legs. Because he'd liked her. Because there'd been some sort of immediate personal connection he couldn't really explain.

Immediate personal connection.

Who was he kidding? He'd been attracted to her.

There was never a more ill-advised person to be attracted to than a woman he'd picked up from the side of the road who was dressed in a bloody wedding gown and didn't even know her own name. No matter how beautiful. No matter how charming or endearing. No matter how great her legs were. And that was all there was to it.

Quinn opened his eyes and sat up to escape the picture of her in his mind and everything it brought with it. Maybe he should just turn this one over to the cops, after all, and stay out of it.

But before he'd decided one way or the other, his brother walked into the emergency room.

Heads turned to Logan just as they did to everyone who entered, but those of the women in the room didn't turn away again. They went on staring, some of them slack jawed.

Mr. Gorgeous in a police uniform. It made Quinn chuckle to himself.

"You pulled uniform duty instead of plain clothes today?" Quinn said in greeting to his brother.

"Disciplinary action for another trumped-up infraction. Wortman is out for my hide," Logan answered with a sharp edge to his voice as he sat in the chair on the other side of the corner table at a ninety-degree angle from Quinn.

"Wortman's a jerk."

"The biggest. Unfortunately he's also my commanding officer."

Logan didn't seem to notice the female gawking aimed his way. Quinn figured his brother was accustomed to it by now.

"So, how's the mystery woman?" Logan asked then.

"You know hospitals. All they'll say is they're running tests. Did you find anything on her?"

Logan shook his head. "There are no missing persons reports filed that fit her description or use the name Cara. She isn't wanted for anything, and there haven't been any stray grooms or wedding disturbances, either. I didn't come up with a single thing, good or bad, that might be a lead to finding out who she is or what happened to her. Looks like she's just another Jane Doe."

Logan hadn't met her or he wouldn't have dismissed her so easily. This woman was special. Quinn could feel it.

Or was that just the attraction talking?

"Will you fingerprint her and see if you can call in a favor from Jackson over at Motor Vehicles to run them?" Quinn asked.

"Sure, but I can't today. I'm off tomorrow. I'll sign out a kit when I get off tonight and do it then. Will she be here?"

"The nurse says it looks like they're going to release her."

Logan grimaced. "Bad time for that. The weather was hot this weekend. You know what that means."

"Tempers ran as high as the temperatures and fists flew. The shelters and safe houses are full," Quinn finished.

Logan nodded. "To the brim. I just called in a social worker who took a woman with two kids to her own place because the only other option was for them to sleep on the floor somewhere else." He glanced toward a doctor at the desk. "If your mystery woman really has amnesia we could probably persuade them to keep her in the psych ward a few days."

This time it was Quinn who grimaced. "That's not pretty."

"It's a bed to sleep in there or a floor in a shelter."

One option was as unpalatable as the other. "What if this were Lindsey?" Quinn said, thinking out loud of their sister.

"I wouldn't want her in either place," Logan agreed.

"I wish Lindsey was in better shape herself right now. I'd see if she'd take Cara in," Quinn said.

"She isn't in good shape, though. The divorce, losing Bobby."

"I know. She isn't even working. She's doing some background checks, minor paperwork, but I've been handling all the cases that come into the agency because she can't deal with anything but trying to put her life back together at the moment. Luckily business is slow."

"Besides, you can't overlook the circumstances around your mystery woman. Whoever shot her—" Logan stalled and backtracked. "Have the doctors confirmed that?"

"I haven't heard, but I've seen enough gunshot wounds to recognize one."

"So, whoever shot her could track her down and try again," Logan finished.

"And Lindsey is as good a P.I. as I am but she's not at top speed now. That'd put them both in danger."

"The same is true of admitting the lady to the psych ward. Whoever she's around could come under the line of fire. And the more overrun the shelters, the weaker the security there, too, so it wouldn't be much better," Logan reflected. Then he said, "What kind of trouble does this woman look like?"

Quinn knew what his brother was thinking. He'd been a cop himself long enough to have seen the worst humanity had to offer, and some people earned what happened to them. "Nah, Cara isn't trouble herself. She's the girl next door. Somebody's sister." Except that his thoughts about her weren't brotherly. "I'd bet my new car she's an innocent victim."

"Why don't you put her up in the guest room at the house, then?"

"I don't know about that," Quinn hedged. The fact that what was churning around inside of him wasn't brotherly was uppermost in his mind. Having her in the bedroom right beside his didn't seem like a good idea.

"You are going to take her case, aren't you?" Logan asked when Quinn was slow to answer his question.

"A *case* is when someone comes to me with a problem and hires me to solve it. I just picked this woman up. She is not a case."

"But she needs help. She needs someone to find out who she is, where she came from, who shot her. And you know where all that falls in the system—right through the cracks. She'll be a file on somebody's desk from now until there aren't any bigger cases or more demanding crimes to solve. In other words, until hell freezes over. She'll just be another displaced person who either makes it on her own starting from scratch without even a name, or she'll end up in the streets. Or worse yet, whoever shot her this time will find her and do a better job of it."

"Okay, okay, tell me something I don't know," Quinn snapped.

"No, you tell me what I don't know. How come you pick up this woman, bring her here, wait for her, call me in on it, but pull back now? That isn't like you."

Quinn glanced off his right shoulder, away from his brother, and muttered under his breath, "I like her."

"You have the hots for her?" Logan rephrased with a laugh.

"No, not the hots," Quinn objected, though getting the hots for her was uncomfortably within the realm of possibility. "But I don't want to get too involved."

"Personally involved," Logan amended. "No, that wouldn't be smart. She'd be a client. And worse than that, a client with amnesia, with no history. No way to know what you could be getting into."

"Exactly."

"So I guess it's the psych ward or a blanket on a shelter's floor."

Quinn ran the backs of his fingers along his jaw in an agitated scratch. Dammit. Why'd he have to think about Lindsey in this situation? About bad things happening when he didn't follow through on things? And now that he had, how the hell could he leave Cara to either of the options?

He sighed disgustedly. Whether at himself or fate, he wasn't sure. "I guess I'll have to keep things under control and take her home with me."

"Think of her as strictly business," Logan advised.

"Right," Quinn answered dubiously, wondering just how to do that with the disarmingly charming Cara.

In the bedroom one door away from his....

CARA FELT considerably better. Napping on the drive from the mountains had helped, but so had the painkiller the doctor had given her for her headache and the shower and shampoo she'd been allowed. Plus all she'd done for four hours was lie down or be pushed in a wheelchair. In fact, she was feeling so much better she was bored.

She sat up and took stock of the room she'd been left in to wait for the results after the last test. It was very small, only large enough for the table she was on, a chair in the corner, a stool with wheels for the doctor and a narrow counter and cupboard for a few instruments and jars of cotton balls, swabs, bandages and tongue depressors.

The door was closed, but she knew from her trip to X-ray that beyond it was the central nurse's station, around which all the examining rooms like this one

opened. From there another door led to the waiting
area.

And Quinn Strummel.

She knew he was still out there because she'd asked.
And that made her feel even better than all the medical attention and rest she'd gotten. It might be crazy,
but he seemed to be her only anchor in this sea of con-
fusion in which she'd found herself.

"I'm as bad as a baby duck bonding to the first thing
it sees when it cracks out of its shell," she murmured
to herself, wondering why she could remember something as inconsequential as that, but not her own name.

Still, it was very reassuring to know he was waiting
for her.

The thought of seeing him again held no small appeal, either, though she knew she shouldn't be foster-
ing sentiments like that. It felt too much like the kind
of anticipation she would feel for a second meeting
with someone she had designs on. Which, of course,
was crazy.

But there it was all the same—a sense of excitement
that he'd stayed, that she would get to see him once
more, this time with clear eyesight since the blurred vision had gone away.

Not that he could look much better.

Who could ask for more than a face as ruggedly
handsome as a Roman gladiator's? Or a body so big
and hard and strong he could pick her up into his arms
as if she were weightless and carry her away like a hero
in an old movie?

Not that she was asking for anything, she amended
as if some greater force might be listening to her
thoughts. It wasn't as if she were looking to start a ro-

mance with him. It was just a rhetorical *who* as in, "Who could ask for more?"

And she trusted him without question now, too. Somewhere along the way she'd lost even the smallest doubts about him. After all, if he meant her any harm he certainly wouldn't have brought her here and put in a call to his brother the police officer before Cara had even been taken back to see a doctor.

No, he was a person of integrity to go along with his good looks, she knew instinctively. Quite a package was Mr. Quinn Strummel, private investigator.

Not that it mattered.

She shouldn't even be thinking about it. It was just that she was so bored.

Her stomach rumbled just then and gave her something else to occupy her thoughts—hunger. She'd kill for a candy bar.

Well, maybe not kill, but she could at least put some effort into getting one.

She slid to the bottom of the examining table and gingerly got down. For a moment she stood there, testing her faculties. She was still dizzy, her head hurt slightly and her balance was only slightly improved. But none of it was as immediately important as her craving for chocolate.

She gathered the overwashed fabric of her hospital gown into a fist behind her so as not to expose her bare rear end through the slit in the back and went to the door, opening it to peer out.

There wasn't a soul in sight, so she ventured to the central nurse's station and stood there, hoping someone would appear at any moment.

When no one did, she again thought of Quinn Strummel, this time in the wholly acceptable context of procurer of candy bars.

She was less eager to poke her head out the door to the waiting area, but a louder, more insistent growl of her stomach persuaded her.

Quinn was out there, all right, one ankle braced on his knee, his arms locked over his broad chest, his head against the wall, eyes closed.

It occurred to her that the only reason he was still there was because he'd fallen asleep instead of going home, that he hadn't been waiting for her, after all.

It was a discouraging thought.

Then Cara reasoned that he'd have left immediately if he hadn't intended to wait and she felt better again.

"Pssst! Mr. Strummel!" she called in a library voice, not wanting to draw any more attention than she had to.

But every chair in the waiting area was occupied, and the only head that didn't turn her way was Quinn's.

"Mr. Strummel?" she tried again.

An elderly gentleman sitting beside Quinn realized who she was trying to rouse. He pointed at Quinn and raised bushy white eyebrows in question.

Cara nodded her head, and the old gentleman tapped Quinn on the shoulder, saying something Cara couldn't hear that opened his eyes and finally made him aware of her. He was up and out of his seat instantly, crossing the area in long, even strides that she found surprisingly graceful for so large a man.

"What are the chances of increasing my debt to you by two candy bars?" she asked when he reached her.

"Feeling better, are we?"

"If starvation doesn't count."

"How's the memory?"

"Still gone in regards to everything but chocolate."

That made him smile and the simple sight of it gave her a tiny thrill she didn't want to acknowledge.

"There's a machine around the corner," he said by way of concession.

"Oh, good. I'm back in room three. I think it's all right if you bring them there."

She ducked behind the door again and returned to the examining room so she could arrange the hospital gown to preserve her modesty before he joined her. By the time he did she was sitting on the edge of the table again, the loose rear flaps of the gown securely underneath her.

"I didn't know what you like so I brought one of each—plain chocolate, chocolate with almonds, chocolate with coconut and chocolate with peanut butter."

"I think I like them all, thanks," she said, accepting them. Then she motioned toward the chair in the corner. "You can sit here if you want. They're done poking me and checking me out and looking at me like I'm an alien from another planet. Now I'm just waiting for the verdict." And she very much wanted his company so she was pleased when he sat down.

She opened the peanut-butter candy first, reasoning that peanut butter was nutritious, and offered him part of it. But she didn't mind that he refused because she was famished. Her only problem was keeping herself from inhaling it.

"So how are you?" he asked.

But she didn't have a chance to answer with more than a shrug of her shoulders before the doctor walked in.

Cara introduced them and let the doctor know she didn't mind if Quinn stayed to hear what he had to say. "Unless you don't want to," she added to Quinn as an afterthought.

"Actually I'd like to," he assured her.

The black-bearded M.D. leaned against the counter and scanned the first of several pages attached to a clipboard. "You have what appears to be a gunshot wound to the head."

Cara glanced to Quinn to give him his due but said, "Are you sure?" because she still found it difficult to believe.

"Reasonably sure, yes," the doctor answered. "You were very lucky. The bullet only grazed you. Still, it could have been enough of a blow to cause the amnesia. Or the amnesia could be a result of shock, perhaps if you were shot by someone close to you, someone you knew and trusted. Amnesia is a tricky business. It's even harder to pinpoint the exact origin in this case, where the damage to the cranium is minor."

"But my memory will come back," she prompted hopefully, opening the second candy bar.

"I can't say that. It could come back at any time or not at all. It could come back only partially. All I can tell you is that there isn't a thing we can do for it."

Cara paused in eating the chocolate, surprised and not happy to hear that. "There isn't a drug to help or anything I can do?"

"Nothing. I'm sorry. If the amnesia is from the head trauma, then we can hope as it heals and any intercranial swelling goes down, you'll regain everything in a matter of a week or two."

"And if it isn't from the injury?" Quinn asked.

"If it's emotional in origin—" the doctor shrugged elaborately "—that's a whole other can of worms. Hypnosis with a reputable psychotherapist might help. But give it some time before getting into anything like that and hope the cause is physical and will take care of itself."

There was something consoling about the chocolate, and Cara opened the third candy bar as he went on.

"Otherwise you're in perfect health," he said, flipping through the pages. "You appear to be about thirty years old, have never borne a child, had your appendix removed probably as a teenager, have a very small heart-shaped tattoo on your right hip—faded enough to have been there since you were a teenager or a very young adult. Your eyesight is twenty-twenty, your hearing is normal, vital stats are normal, blood is normal and you have four fillings in your teeth," he concluded.

"No doubt from the chocolate," Quinn muttered as she demurely devoured the final confection.

The doctor crossed his arms over the clipboard to hold it to his chest. "I don't see any reason to keep you here," he said, leaving a pregnant pause after it.

Cara realized then that since awakening in the meadow she hadn't given any thought to anything but the moment. She hadn't considered the eventuality of being sent on her way. On her way to nowhere. A wave of panic rushed through her.

But before it completely overtook her, Quinn said, "It's all right. You can stay at my place."

Relief and gratitude were Cara's first reactions. Then something else occurred to her that threatened the small sense of connection she felt to him. "Will that be all right with your wife, or whoever you live with?'' she asked hesitantly, hating that he might assure her his wife or live-in lover wouldn't mind a bit.

"I don't have a wife and I live alone. But I do have a guest room, with a lock on the door, in case you were worried. And my brother the cop lives in the carriage house out back, so you'll have sort of a chaperon."

Cara was just happy to know he wasn't married or living with a woman. The rest didn't matter in her newfound trust of him.

The doctor pushed away from the counter, clearly relieved that he wouldn't be releasing her with no-where to go. "I'll donate a pair of surgical scrubs for you to wear and you can be on your way then. Get a couple of days' rest, take any over-the-counter pain reliever for the headache and call me if you have problems. Other than that—'' he shrugged again ''—all I can say is good luck."

QUINN TOLD CARA on the way out of the hospital that his house was in a section of north Denver. It didn't mean anything at all to her, and not a single thing looked familiar as they drove there, even though she tried hard to recognize anything at all—the highway they traveled, Denver's skyline in the distance, the quiet neighborhood streets with houses that sat far back from the roads, even the scent and feel of the air or the way the stars looked close enough to touch. But nothing stirred a memory. Whether because of the amnesia or because she wasn't from Colorado at all, she didn't know.

Quinn's house was a two-story red brick with a steep roof and a big front porch. Elm and oak trees marked the sides of his property and more grew in the back.

The trees spoke of decades, growing well above the roofs, their branches all meeting overhead to mix and mingle and form a canopy of leaves.

"What month is it?" Cara asked as he pulled into the drive that ran alongside the house and into the garage that was the lower half of what he'd called the carriage house. The upper half was where his brother lived.

"Today is the first of September." He went on to fill her in on the year and who was president as they got out of the car, but none of it rang a bell for her.

"May I call you Quinn?" she asked on the way through a backyard of manicured lawn and flower gardens.

"What else would you call me?" he asked a little gruffly as he unlocked the rear door.

"Mr. Strummel. That's what I called you when I tried to get your attention at the hospital before that old man woke you."

"Just Quinn is fine." He pushed open the door, flipped on a light and held the screen for her, keeping the large plastic trash bag that contained her wedding dress and underwear out of the way so she could go in ahead of him.

"Maybe I do something that requires formality, since it came naturally. Maybe I work in a funeral home," she guessed with a tinge of dread in her voice.

The gruffness disappeared in a chuckle at her. "There are plenty of other places where people are formal. How about a bank?"

"Or maybe I'm an emissary to foreign dignitaries," she suggested more enthusiastically.

He grinned at her. "Can you speak any other languages?"

She thought about it. "Not that I can remember."

"I don't think it's likely that you're an emissary to foreign dignitaries in Denver, anyway."

"Spoilsport." She went into a small, neat laundry room and then turned left into the kitchen just ahead of Quinn, who reached a long arm over her shoulder to turn a light on there, too. When he did, she again caught a whiff of his after-shave. Heady stuff. She breathed deeply and enjoyed.

Her first impression of his kitchen was that it was warm and homey and somehow masculine. There was an abundance of oak cupboards, and aged red brick on most of the walls. The countertops were cream-and-tan marble, except for the center island which had a cutting board on either side of the five-burner stove top. Over the island hung a cast-iron cache rack lined with copper pots and pans. Very French country, she thought, though it was something else she didn't know how she knew.

"Maybe I'm an interior decorator," she murmured. "I like your kitchen."

"Maybe you're a chef."

She considered that, but somehow it didn't seem as if she had a feel for food. "I don't think so. Chocolate is the only thought I have of anything edible."

"I guess that leaves it up to me to fix something for us to eat besides candy bars." He set the bag in a corner and went to the refrigerator, saying along the way, "You're in luck—I make a great sandwich and I have everything we need."

"Can I help?"

"No, I solo in the kitchen. Why don't you just sit down and take it easy?"

She was too curious to do that, wondering about him, about this place, about what might summon a memory of something. She wandered to the open doorway that led to the rest of the house, peering through it as if across a gulch.

"You can look around if you want," Quinn offered. "Just don't head upstairs by yourself if you're still dizzy. We've spent enough time at that hospital for one day." Then he added as an afterthought, "Oh, and I can't guarantee that you'll find things too clean. I didn't expect to come home with company."

Steadying herself with a hand against the wall, she wandered from the kitchen into the hall that seemed to connect it to the rest of the house. She found a small bathroom and then looked into the second doorway down from it.

"That's the office of Strummel Investigations," Quinn called.

It was a large room that looked to have been two combined. Inside the paneled confines were desks, a few visitor's chairs, a sofa, filing cabinets, a computer and printer and space to spare. It seemed like a normal, if very large, in-home office, though Cara wasn't sure what she'd expected—maybe wanted posters on the walls or guns hanging from holsters on a hall tree.

Silly, she supposed, but then her idea of a private detective came from movies and television, though she couldn't pinpoint anything specific, just a general image of larger-than-life men in action on big or small screens.

Down the parquet-floored hall she encountered the stairs and a small entranceway at the front of the house. The door there was old and solid, carved with an intricate design of leaves and vines. Very beautiful.

To the right was the living room, and Cara went into it, finding a light switch that turned on two table lamps on either side of an overstuffed leather couch. Her bare feet sank into thick shag carpet the color of coffee with cream.

This was definitely a man's house. The only knickknacks were an array of remote controls on the pedestal coffee table and a half dozen sports magazines.

But somehow Cara found that nice—not the litter, but the feel of masculinity in the dark brown armchair that matched the sofa and the absence of anything too frilly.

That she should like that seemed incongruous with the little she knew about herself, specifically that her wedding gown had been very ornate. Garishly so. In fact she'd really hated it when she'd peeled it off and taken a good look at it. It had ruffles and flounces everywhere that ruffles and flounces could possibly have been.

No, this more sedate, practical style was very appealing to her. Maybe because it spoke so strongly of Quinn and not because of any change that had happened in her taste in the last few hours, although any change in the taste that had chosen that wedding gown was an improvement.

There was a fireplace with a carved mantel very similar to the front door, both probably antiques, and an impressive oak entertainment center filled with a large TV, a VCR and several pieces of stereo equipment to go with all the remote controls. There was also a chessboard on a table in front of a big picture window and a wall of bookcases.

Wondering what Quinn's taste in reading material was, she went to one of the bookcases. Police procedurals, forensic manuals, a number of informational books and journals kept company with books on human psychology. There were philosophy books, too—Kant, Kierkegaard, Nietzsche. And then there was the fiction section—mysteries, intrigue and a healthy collection of Westerns.

The Westerns made her smile. Being a P.I. seemed a little like being a modern-day Wyatt Earp, and she wondered if his love for them had influenced his choice in careers.

There were also a few trophies and plaques displayed in the bookcase. Quinn had been an all-star quarterback in high school and a Golden Gloves boxer in college, as well as an outstanding police officer who had excelled in the line of duty. His badge was there, too, framed against blue velvet the color of a uniform.

It made Cara wonder why he'd stopped being something he'd not only been good at but had clearly been proud of.

"Did you get lost out here?"

Cara jumped at the sound of Quinn's voice from the arched entrance to the room.

"I'm sorry," he said quickly, "I didn't mean to scare you. I thought you heard me come in."

"It's okay," she assured, though her heart was beating a mile a minute.

"Everything is ready. We can eat."

But his previous career was still on her mind and she nodded toward the mementos. "How come you quit being a police officer?"

He didn't answer immediately, and when he finally did, what he said was no answer at all. "It's a long story. I'll tell you sometime. But right now we need to concentrate on you and getting something in your stomach that isn't chocolate.''

Did that mean the reason he left the police force was unimportant? Or too important to talk about with a stranger? His hesitancy only increased her interest, but there wasn't anything she could do to soothe it, so Cara merely said okay and moved away from the bookcase to follow him back to the kitchen.

It was a good distraction. He had a great walk with just enough swagger to it to say he was a man to be reckoned with. And though he had a calendar-perfect derriere, it was his shoulders that Cara liked best— broad, square shoulders that would have made him an imposing force even if he weren't so tall. She liked the way his hair waved against his collar, too, just long enough to prove him a touch unconventional while showing he wasn't overly concerned with appearance, or much of a perfectionist, either—things that appealed to her for no reason she understood.

He'd set two places at the round, claw-footed table that took up the dining room section of the kitchen. There was plate of sandwiches in the center, a bowl of chips, one of black olives and another of green grapes.

''I didn't know what you'd want to drink—milk, water, tea, coffee, cola. Take your pick.''

She didn't know what she drank, either, but of those choices only water or tea sounded good. He was having iced tea, so she opted for that. He laced his with a lemon wedge and brought the sugar bowl for her.

''I know, you figured I have a terrible sweet tooth because of the candy bars,'' she guessed. ''But I think it's the chocolate I like because sweet stuff that isn't chocolate doesn't appeal to me.''

She took a sandwich then, realizing at the sight of it just how hungry she was again. And he was right, he made a terrific concoction of an assortment of meats and cheeses, lettuce, tomato, pickles, mayonnaise and just a hint of French mustard. It was so thick she could barely squeeze it into her mouth to take a bite.

"My brother was at the hospital," he told her after he'd tasted his food, going on to relay what he'd said. "Logan—that's his name—will come over tomorrow and fingerprint you. We might be able to turn up a driver's license for you that way."

"What if I'm not from here? Will it help find one from another state if I just came to Denver to get married?"

He shook his head until he'd swallowed what was in his mouth. "No, I'm sorry to say it won't. You'll have to have a Colorado license for it to come up. Or a police record."

She stopped with a potato chip midway to her lips. "Do you think I have a police record?"

He laughed. "No, I don't, or I wouldn't have brought you into my home. I'm just telling you what the possibilities are."

"I thought maybe you just took in all the stray amnesiacs you found on roadsides," she bantered back, surprised by the flirtatious sound of her own voice.

"You're the first."

It pleased her that he'd made an exception to help her but she didn't want it to show. "Are you the only detective in Strummel Investigations?"

"No, my sister Lindsey is a P.I., too."

"Your sister?"

"Mmm-hmm. But she isn't doing much at the moment. She's had some personal problems and she's taking time off to regroup."

One thing Cara was learning about herself was that she was nosy. General answers like that and the earlier one about why he'd left the police force were very unsatisfying. Still, as before, she didn't think she should pursue it. "Do you have other brothers or sisters? Parents?"

"No other brothers or sisters. But we do have parents. They moved to Seattle when they retired." He glanced around the room. "This house was theirs until then. I bought it from them."

"You grew up here?"

"Yes, I did."

Cara had eaten her fill and pushed her plate away. "You said the cabin you were at in the mountains belonged to your family. Does that mean you bought it from your parents, too?"

"No, as a matter of fact they never owned it. Logan, Lindsey and I pooled our resources to buy it." He paused and shook his head wryly. "Speaking of families, has anything at all come back to you?"

"Not a thing," she said wearily, realizing that was how she felt, too. "Maybe after a night's sleep . . ."

"Are you about ready for that? You seem to be wilting before my eyes."

"I guess that makes me a rude houseguest. Add it to the list of little-knowns about Cara Whatever-my-name-is."

"It doesn't make you a rude houseguest, just a not completely well one," he amended. He seemed to have finished eating and pushed his chair away from the table to get to his feet. "Come on, I'll show you your room."

"I'll help you clean this up first."

"Not a chance." He pulled her chair out and took her elbow to help her stand, but the gruffness came back into his voice then, as if to roughen up the edges of his consideration. "All I need is you keeling over with a knife in your hand."

She wasn't sure whether she required his assistance or not, but it felt too good to have that capable hand on her bare arm to protest, and she really was too tired to argue any more about doing the dishes, so instead she let him take her to the stairs.

Once they were there he stood aside for her to go up first. "I'll follow you and keep hold of your waist just in case," he informed her.

"I think I'll be okay if I just hang on to the railing," she said demurely.

"You're weak and still weaving when you walk. I don't want to take the chance."

She headed up the steps and by the third one she was glad to have his help, and not only because she needed it. The warmth of his hands on either side of her seeped through the thin fabric of the surgical scrubs she wore and suffused her with a pleasure she didn't want to admit even to herself, along with bolstering both her strength and her spirits. And they needed bolstering for, somehow, facing the night suddenly made her present predicament feel very weighty.

He must have been able to tell how sapped were the resources that had served her up until then, because at the landing to the upper level he only let go of her with one hand, keeping the other at her waist as he came up beside her so that his arm stretched across the small of her back.

"My room is here." He pointed to the first door on the right, then moved her to the next one down. "And this is yours. The bathroom is on the other side of the hall."

He guided her into a plain, cream-colored room with a single five-drawer bureau and a matching double bed that looked downy between the four spindled posts that poked two feet above the mattress at each corner. The only other furniture in the room was a small desk with a chair that had seen good use.

"I'll get you one of my T-shirts to sleep in. There's a new toothbrush in the top dresser drawer, and towels in the linen closet in the bathroom."

He disappeared, and while he was gone she crossed to the window and pulled the shade from behind the swag valance that added a cozy touch to the otherwise Spartan room. Then she pressed down on the quilt-covered bed to see if it really was as soft as it looked. It was and she ached to climb into it.

Quinn was back again in a moment, standing before her, offering a navy blue, V-necked T-shirt that would fit her like a dress, and a black terry-cloth bathrobe that obviously also belonged to him.

"Thanks," she said, accepting them. Then she added, "For everything."

He cleared his throat as if he were uneasy about something and looked away from her. "You're welcome," he said under his breath. Then, very efficiently, he added, "Like I said at the hospital, there's a lock on the door. Use it if it makes you feel better. If you need anything during the night, just call. I'm a light sleeper."

She nodded and he turned to go.

"Quinn?"

He faced her again, his eyebrows pulled together in a questioning frown.

"Why do you suppose no one reported me missing?"

Something softened slightly in his expression, maybe because her tone had given away the vulnerability and doubt that had so suddenly come over her. He reached a halting hand to the side of her neck, clearly meaning only to comfort and reassure her. "Let's not jump to any conclusions."

But there was more than comfort in the contact of his palm against her skin. At least it did more than comfort her. It sent a scattershot of sparks raining through her that had nothing at all to do with solace.

She looked up into his eyes and found them shining silver, penetrating hers in a way that made her think she wasn't the only one feeling what she was feeling and that it had taken him off guard, too.

Then he let her go and put some distance between them in a hurry.

"Get some rest. Everything will look better in the morning," he said in a husky voice, leaving the room on three long strides and closing the door firmly behind him.

And even though Cara knew it was the craziest thing to happen in what had to be one of the most insane days of her life, she couldn't help basking in the warm afterglow of his touch.

Chapter Three

Quinn was up early the following morning. He started coffee and then ran to the convenience store for the newspapers that weren't delivered to his house. By the time he'd gone through those and the ones that arrived on his front porch, he had to brew a second pot.

But he hadn't come across a single item that seemed as if Cara could be connected to it.

He stacked the papers in the center of the kitchen table and sat back, staring at them and remembering her question the night before about why no one had reported her missing.

He had a couple of theories.

It was possible that everyone who knew her thought she was away on a happy honeymoon. Everyone except her groom. And of the two reasons her groom wouldn't have notified the police, neither was good.

It was possible that she and her new husband had left their wedding, met up with some creep or creeps and he'd been victimized, too.

But it could also be that her groom was the one who shot her and left her in the hills where he believed no one would find her until it was too late.

If Quinn were to bet on a scenario, the second of those theories was where he'd put his money.

Still, though, he couldn't ignore that first one. And it put a spotlight on another reason why his attraction to Cara was so out-of-bounds—it could be that she was happily married. And it was also possible that her husband would crop up just the way she had—injured, but still alive and kicking and ready to take back his bride.

In the meantime Quinn needed to keep his distance. He needed to control the attraction he felt for her.

He sure as hell didn't need to be thinking about kissing her the way he had been last night before he'd left her in her room.

That had to go down as one of the most inane urges in history.

And one of the most overwhelming.

He should never have touched her. Looking at her, listening to her, stirred up things inside of him, but he'd been ignoring them and that had helped keep them at bay. But then there she'd been, suddenly uncertain and vulnerable, and dammit all to hell, he'd melted.

There was some sort of chemistry between them that was combustible.

Her silky, bourbon-colored hair had fallen over his hand, her skin had been so warm and soft, she'd looked up at him with those incredible violet eyes that were the color of a clear sky just before nightfall, and the next thing he knew he was imagining what it would be like to pull her into his arms, to feel her small breasts against his chest, to taste that mouth that was so supple it drove him a little wild....

Just remembering what had gone through his mind made sweat break out on his upper lip even as he sat there at his kitchen table.

But she was off-limits.

He had to maintain a purely professional relationship with her. He had to start thinking of her as a client. Only a client. With a whole life waiting for her out there somewhere. A life she'd go back to. A life that probably came complete with a husband.

He had to squash any personal interest or involvement with her before it got out of hand.

And that meant he sure as hell couldn't kiss her.

No matter how much he might want to.

THE SMALL ALARM CLOCK on the nightstand said 12:16 when Cara woke up. She knew immediately where she was and what had happened to her in the previous twenty-four hours. But as she lay in bed and did a mental scan for anything else, she found she still had no memory leading up to that.

She did remember a dream she'd had during the night, though. A very vivid dream of walking up to a house, going in, looking around. There were no people in the dream, but the place had given her a sense of home, of peace and security, of welcome.

Unfortunately there was nothing in the dream or in her memory that told her where the house was. But it was nice to wake with a lingering of those good feelings.

Actually, she realized as she got up, she felt good all the way around after her long sleep.

There was still a dull ache in her head, but nothing too serious, and beyond that everything else was great. The dizziness was gone, she had her balance back, she felt refreshed and rejuvenated and ready to take on the world.

With Quinn's help.

She also craved a long, hot bath.

She poked her head out the bedroom door to see if the coast was clear, and when she discovered it was, she took Quinn's robe and padded across the hall to the bathroom.

Her yearning for a long soak was so strong that she made quick work of ridding herself of the T-shirt she wore and stepped into the modern, oversize black tub even before she turned on the water. Then, when she had, she lay back and closed her eyes until she was nearly chin deep in the steamy stuff and what was coming out of the faucet was cool.

Bliss. It felt so wonderful that she didn't even care that a good houseguest would never have used up all the hot water. She was finding that things like the invigoration of a morning bath, the taste of chocolate, the smell of autumn in the air, the sight of bright sunshine, brought with them a comforting familiarity that she yearned to soak up and savor.

Had she always found such pleasure in small things, or was it just the satisfaction of having at least a few visceral memories?

She didn't know. But whatever the reason, she indulged guiltlessly until the water cooled too much to be comfortable anymore.

Standing to dry off, she studied each part of her body as she did, relearning it—the shape of her legs, the indentation of her waist, the upturn of her breasts.

The tattoo on her hip gave her pause. She wondered if it meant she'd been a wild, rebellious teenager. Or did it mean something else? Maybe her last name was Heart.

"Cara Heart," she said aloud, trying it out.

It didn't sound right to her so she discarded the idea and went back to wondering about what had led her to get herself tattooed. Maybe she was a hard-living woman trucker or a motorcycle mama or maybe she was just in the habit of throwing caution to the wind and doing flamboyant things.

Not unappealing images of herself, she decided. In fact she liked the idea that she might be a little outrageous.

When she was completely dry she stepped out of the tub and up to the sink.

"The unveiling," she murmured to herself with mock drama as she used the towel to clear the steam-clouded mirror so she could have her first look at her face now, too.

There hadn't been a mirror in the shower at the hospital, and the single time she'd used this bathroom the night before she'd been too tired to care what she looked like. But now she was anxious.

"Here goes. Drumroll, please," she said when she'd finally dried the glass.

But it wasn't her face she saw reflected back at her.

Or anything else, really.

That initial glimpse into the mirror brought with it a sudden, intense sense of dread and a sort of mental blip that blocked out everything else in a split second's flash.

She closed her eyes and let her head hang lower than her shoulders, taking deep breaths, waiting for her heart to stop racing so fast she could hear it, willing away the sickening spin inside her head.

A dizzy spell, she thought. *That's all it was.*

But did dizzy spells bring with them such over-whelming emotions?

When the physical sensations subsided she slowly raised her head and glanced in the mirror again, almost afraid of a rerun.

But it didn't happen. Her eyes finally focused and there in the glass was only her face against the back-drop of the bathroom.

"It must have just been a dizzy spell," she said to herself, sure of it now.

She took one more deep breath, sighed it out and leaned in closer to the mirror to finally have that look at her own face.

As with the sensory things, there was a certain vague familiarity as she gazed at herself. It was an accepta-ble face, she decided. It would have been nice to find a smaller nose and fuller lips, but at least she had high cheekbones and her eyes were a good color.

Did she use makeup? she wondered.

Her skin was clear but a little pale, and her eye-lashes were okay but nothing mascara couldn't im-prove.

And then there was her hair. It was all one length, several inches lower than her shoulders, and the color of cinnamon sticks. Not too thin, not too thick or coarse. But it was strange to look at it and not know how she wore it.

Did she curl it in coquettish cascades? Did she tie it at her nape like a schoolteacher? Or wrap it into a bun like a librarian? Did she braid it like a farm girl? Or put it in a ponytail or a Gibson girl knot or leave it hang-ing loosely down her back?

Then it occurred to her that it didn't really matter what she'd done with it before.

In a way, amnesia was a clean slate. She could reinvent herself. Start over from scratch and do whatever she felt like.

And not only with her hair. As long as she didn't have a past or any expectations of her or any demands or roles to fill, she was perfectly free.

And it felt good. It felt very good.

"Maybe I'm escaping oppression," she said melodramatically, not really believing it.

All she knew was that as long as things stood the way they did—dizzy spells notwithstanding—she might as well enjoy it.

For some reason what popped into her mind with that was the image of Quinn.

"Shame on you," she told her reflection.

But it didn't help. Especially when she slipped into his bathrobe and the clean scent of him wrapped around her as surely as the terry cloth.

The smell caused an instant mental replay of those moments just before he'd left her the night before. Of the feel of his hand on her skin. Of the look in his eyes—

She cut the indulgence short and reminded herself that enjoying the temporary freedom from being whoever she was didn't mean enjoying Quinn Strummel in any but the most platonic ways. She was in no position to be thinking about what it might feel like to have his arms around her or to run her palms up his biceps to the wide span of his shoulders, or any of the rest of what was in her mind at that moment. She was in no position to be having the feelings she was having, either, the desire to do just what she was imagining. And she absolutely had to put a stop to it all.

"Don't you have enough to sort through?" she asked her reflection.

Of course she did. More than enough.

So she wasn't going to entertain any more of those thoughts. Or desires. She absolutely was not.

But even good intentions couldn't take away how eager she was to get downstairs to him.

THERE WERE TWO male voices coming from the kitchen when Cara descended the steps a half hour later. She'd carefully combed her hair over the crease left by her wound and braided only the last three inches of it to keep it out of her face. She'd also pinched her cheeks to put some color into them, but that was about all she could do in the way of a toilette. She still wore Quinn's bathrobe, carrying the surgical scrubs with her as she went on silent bare feet down the hall.

Neither of the men noticed her when she first stepped into the doorway. Quinn sat at the table while another man rinsed a coffee cup at the sink and put it in the dishwasher.

The other man was tall and muscular and had Quinn's same ruggedly distinctive features, only they were more refined. Where Quinn was very handsome, this man was drop-dead gorgeous. The guy could have stepped out of a magazine ad.

But when Cara's gaze moved from him to Quinn, it was Quinn who put her heart into fibrillation.

"Good morning," he said when he saw her. "Or I guess I should say good afternoon."

"Hi," she greeted in return, going toward him as if he were her energy source.

Quinn nodded at the other man, who was looking at Cara so carefully she felt as if he were hiring her for a job. "This is my brother Logan. We've just been waiting for you." Then to the Adonis, "Logan, this is Cara...?"

She shrugged. "Sorry. Sleep didn't refresh my memory." She let go of her bundle of clothes with one hand and offered it to Logan as he joined them. "It's nice to meet you."

Logan's smile was as picture perfect as the rest of him as they exchanged amenities.

Then Cara returned her attention to Quinn and motioned to the surgical scrubs she held against her waist. "I couldn't make myself put these on again. They smell like the hospital. Could we wash them and get rid of it, do you think?"

"Sure. But you don't have to wear them unless you want to. My sister leaves a pair of tennis shoes and a change of clothes here and she's about your size. I thought you could wear her things until we get you some of your own." He pointed a long index finger at a pair of jeans, a chambray shirt and white sneakers on the island counter, then stood and took the bundle from her to set on the washing machine in the laundry room.

When he came back he said, "Sit down and I'll fix you something to eat while Logan fingerprints you."

Something about the sound of that made her laugh. "And then we'll have coffee over the mug shots," she added.

"How's the head?" Logan asked as he opened a box and took out an ink pad and a strip of paper with a designated square for each finger.

"With the exception of a pretty weird dizzy spell I'm a lot better all the way around."

"But not a hint of your memory returned?" Quinn asked from where he was breaking eggs into a bowl.

"Nothing. Yesterday and a dream I had last night are perfectly clear, but beyond that I'm still completely blank."

"What was the dream about?" Quinn asked.

She told them, explaining the feelings that had come with it and even lingered after she'd gotten up.

Logan pressed her thumb onto the ink pad and then to the paper. "Can you describe the house?"

"It was an old place, two storied, built with dark, rough-looking stones instead of bricks. It sat on a corner, I think, because I could see a house on one side of it but not on the other, and there were a lot of big trees around—like your neighborhood, actually. There was a turret or a tower of some kind right in front, on one corner, and that's where the door was, so it was at an angle to the rest of the house. It was a strange sort of place, someone's idea of a minicastle, I guess. But I liked it."

Logan stopped after taking only three of her fingerprints to glance at Quinn, who met his look.

"There's a place like that over on the corner of Hoyt and Fifty-fourth at the light," Quinn said, as if he were reading his brother's thoughts.

Cara laughed in amazement this time. "You mean it's a real place and you know where it is?"

"It's a real place. We drove past it last night on the way home. It's just off the highway on the main road to this area."

"She could have seen it then," Logan said, "and not really taken note of it consciously, but conjured it up in her subconscious to dream about it."

Cara had to admit that seemed more likely than that she might be from somewhere not far from here.

"Won't hurt to check it out, though," Quinn said.

"Do you know the people there?" she asked him.

He shook his head. "It isn't all that close to here. We just have to pass it to get to and from the highway. I probably wouldn't have noticed it except that there's a light on that corner and I get stopped there pretty often."

"So what will we do?" she asked, barely keeping the excitement out of her voice. "Stake it out and watch who comes and goes to see if I recognize anyone? Maybe sneak up and peek in the windows when everybody leaves?"

This time it was Quinn who laughed while Logan fought it. "I thought we'd go up to the front door, ring the bell and ask if anybody there knows you."

Cara didn't take offense to their finding her humorous. "Well, that's no fun," she chastised, laughing a little herself. "This could be the only adventure of my life and you want to do something as mundane as ring the doorbell?"

"Is this the adventure of your life?" Quinn asked skeptically.

"Seems like it. Here I am with amnesia of all things, getting fingerprinted, being investigated by a real-life detective. Feels like an adventure to me."

"She has a point," Logan said with amusement in his voice as he finished taking her fingerprints and repacked the box.

Cara went to the sink to wash her hands.

"I'm going to take off," Logan said. "I need to get these prints to Jackson so he can have them to work on when he gets the chance. It'll take a while. He has to do the search on his own time. Cara, I enjoyed meeting you."

She returned the sentiment.

"Think about what I said," Quinn called to him as he headed for the back door. "Lindsey and I could use another partner."

That stirred Cara's curiosity, but Quinn didn't let her in on what he'd meant and she didn't want to pry.

He was adeptly chopping onions, peppers and mushrooms when she had dried her hands and went to stand beside him at the island counter. "Can I do something?"

"Pour yourself a cup of coffee and take it with you to that stack of newspapers in the middle of the table. I've been through them already to see if anything looked like it might be connected. Nothing seems to be. There isn't even a wedding announcement with your name or any derivative of it, or the name Peter, either. But I'd like you to go through page by page and see if an article or something might click for you."

"I'll skip the coffee—it sounds awful—but I think I can handle reading newspapers," she said, leaving his side. It was for the best because just being that near to him brought her nerve endings straining to the surface of her skin.

Still, it wasn't easy to concentrate on articles that meant nothing to her while Quinn was in the room. He had on a pair of faded jeans that fitted his every bulging muscle and terrific derriere, and a pink polo shirt that the sheer power of his masculinity managed to make look like the perfect color for a man.

He was clean shaven and impeccably groomed in that way of his that said he did it without vanity, and Cara found herself much more eager to watch him cooking her breakfast than to read about tax hikes. She was struggling with it when he brought two plates of scrambled eggs, bacon and toast to the table and joined her.

"Your breakfast, my lunch," he informed. "Anything striking a familiar note?" he asked then, nodding to the paper.

"Not a thing. It's as if I was literally born yesterday." She tasted her eggs. "Good," she judged, pointing at them with her fork before taking a second bite.

"Keep looking while you eat," he urged, motioning to the papers.

"Are we going to the house in my dreams when we finish eating?" she asked as she did.

"You're supposed to rest, remember?"

"I don't need to, though. I'm rarin' to go."

"Rarin'?" he repeated with a laugh.

"Maybe I'm a cowgirl. All I know is I don't feel like sitting around staring at the walls just because I have a bump on the head. Let's do some detecting," she suggested without suppressing how intriguing she thought it would be.

He stared at her as if assessing if she really was up to going out. After a moment he conceded. "Okay, then we'll check out the house you described, see where that leads us, and when we're finished with that, if you still feel up to it, we'll hit the shopping mall to get you a few essentials and see if we can dig up a lead on your wedding dress. It's one of the few things we can do on a Sunday."

"A lead on the wedding dress?" she repeated.

"If we can get an idea of who sells that brand, we can canvas the stores and try to find out who bought it, if it was delivered, something that will put us on a trail to you."

"It's as easy as that?"

He breathed a wry chuckle. "Only if it works."

"But it doesn't always?"

"Why do you sound hopeful that it won't?" he asked, sounding slightly suspicious.

"It isn't that I hope it won't," she hedged. "It's just that I wouldn't mind if solving this doesn't happen too quickly."

Those piercing eyes of his bored into her for a moment, and Cara wasn't sure if the increase in her pulse was over him or the fact that he seemed to be wondering if she might be trying to put one over on him.

Apparently he opted for not believing the worst of her because he said, "Let me guess—you're all set for car chases and shoot-outs and close escapes down dark alleys. I hate to disappoint you, but we aren't likely to get into anything like that even if finding out who you are takes a while."

"How about treachery and intrigue? Any chance for them?"

He rolled his eyes but seemed to be fighting a smile in spite of himself. "I suppose there's always the possibility of treachery and intrigue."

"Are you just saying that to get me excited?" She hadn't meant that to sound suggestive but that's how it had come out.

"Is that all it takes?" he countered, a slow, sexy smile breaking through his reserve. And just that quick the air between them was charged with the same sparks as the night before.

"I don't know if that's all it takes or not. I have amnesia, remember?" she bantered back, knowing she shouldn't and at the same time wondering if maybe she wasn't just a natural flirt.

His eyes held hers for a moment more, looking like molten silver, before he cleared his throat and nodded at all that was in front of her. "Eat your breakfast and look through the papers so we can get going today," he ordered, sounding very much like the cop he'd once been.

But Cara had the impression his take-charge gruffness was only a cover-up.

THERE WAS NO DOUBT in Cara's mind that the house in her dream and the one Quinn pulled up in front of an hour later were one and the same. Whether or not she'd seen it any time before the previous night on her way to his place was impossible for her to say.

"So, what do we do, present me at the door and ask if I live here?" she wondered out loud as he turned off the engine.

"Pretty much."

"And what if I do? Will you just hand me over and say, 'See you around'?" That possibility didn't sit well with her. It wasn't that she felt fearful. Her sense of this house had been too positive for it to scare her. And it wasn't the same sort of dread she'd felt at the first glance in the mirror, either, so she didn't have the feeling that she was loath to go back to her real life if this was where it was.

And yet something left her seriously unenthusiastic.

She hated to admit it even to herself, but the cause seemed to be the thought that within moments her association with Quinn could be over.

It seemed absolutely nuts, but the moment she thought about him, she knew he was the cause of her reluctance to go up to that house and find out if it was where she belonged.

Not that it had anything to do with anything like an attraction to him, she reasoned quickly. It went back to the baby-duck-bonding theory of the day before. She was convinced of it. He was just a symbol of security, was all.

Wasn't it?

Cara had been so lost in her own silent debate that she was late in realizing Quinn didn't jump in with an answer to her question about him leaving her there.

Finally he said, "Let's just play it by ear."

His tone left her unsure if he was anxious to see the last of her or if even discovering this was her home didn't necessarily mean he would wash his hands of her. But she didn't have time to ask before he got out of the car and rounded it to open her door.

The sense of coming home was strong in Cara as they went up the walk. It was so strong that for a fleeting moment she thought she smelled the aroma of Thanksgiving turkey wafting from the house. But there was no real scent in the air. And she reminded herself that this was September, not November.

Quinn rang the bell when they climbed the three steps to the cement porch that was abutted on both sides by well-tended bushes. A woman who looked to be midthirties opened the door. She had drab brown hair, a plain face and a baby on her hip. Leaving the screen closed, she peered out at them through it, her eyebrows raised in query and not a hint of recognition in her expression.

Quinn introduced himself and immediately showed her his driver's license and one of his cards, holding them against the screen, which she made no move to open. Then he replaced them in his wallet as he introduced Cara as his client. "I'd like you to take a good look at her and tell us if she seems familiar to you?"

The woman frowned, appearing confused, curious and skeptical all at once, but she stared straight at Cara for the first time.

Cara smiled and felt like an idiot.

"I don't know her," the woman said to Quinn as if Cara were only a picture instead of a living, breathing, hearing human being.

Then she glanced back and caught Cara peeking around her at the inside of the house, and annoyance and suspicion appeared in a frown. She reached down and locked the screen door.

"Can you tell us how long you've lived in this house?" Quinn asked, anyway, still in an even tone that was a cross between friendly and authoritative.

"Nearly four years," she said, as if that ended the conversation. She took a step backward and reached for the door.

"Can you give me the name of the people you bought the house from?" Quinn persisted.

"We rent." Now the woman was verging on anger, and the door was halfway shut.

Cara considered blurting out her story in hopes that the woman might be more cooperative, but considered that Quinn knew what he was doing. Besides, her story was a little hard to believe and it seemed likely to make the woman all the more leery of two strangers showing up on her doorstep like this.

"We'll need to know who you rent from," Quinn informed her, anyway, as if she had no choice in the matter. "This is very important and I assure you it won't involve you in anything beyond this."

The woman scowled at him, and it was clear she was debating whether to comply or slam the door in their faces. But Quinn was an imposing person, and in the end, Cara thought, that prevailed.

"We leased the house through the Golden Leaf Rental Agency and that's all I can tell you," she finally said.

It won her a rewarding smile from him. "Thank you," he said just before the door closed them out and the sound of locks being engaged let them know what the woman thought of them.

Quinn took Cara's elbow and they left the porch.

"Well, I guess that was a wild-goose chase," she said. "Even what I could see of the inside of the house wasn't what was in my dream. I feel pretty silly." But she also felt relieved that he wasn't taking this walk back to his car alone, though she didn't want to say that. Or feel it, for that matter.

"Relax. We don't know yet if it was a wild-goose chase. And even if it was, in this business you hit a lot of dead ends for every road that leads somewhere."

As if he realized belatedly that he had hold of her arm, he let go before he went on talking. "It's possible you lived here before, that she just didn't know it. We aren't beaten yet. And think of it this way—you've officially had a door slammed in your face. This is *real* detective work."

The flair in his voice made her laugh and helped her ignore the disappointment that had washed through her when he'd taken his hand away. "So next we go to the rental agency?" she guessed.

"Right. If you're still feeling good enough."

"I'm great," she said with enough vigor to prove it.

They reached the car and he held the door for her before going around to the driver's side. As he did she thought of how she had smelled turkey on the way up the walk to a house she'd probably never seen until driving by it the previous night.

So what do we have here? she thought. *Looking in the mirror scares me, I smell smells that don't exist, dream that houses I've only passed on the street are home and have to fight being attracted to a man who's nearly a perfect stranger when I could well be either a newlywed or on the verge of marrying some other man.*

It was quite a package, she thought with a measure of Quinn's wryness.

Maybe she was Cara the Nutcase.

THE RENTAL AGENCY proved to be just another dead end. It functioned on behalf of the owners of the house who were a conglomerate of investors from out of state, and there were no records on previous tenants.

That left the mall.

Quinn told Cara he chose the Cherry Creek Shopping Center because it was centrally located and had a specialty bridal salon, as well as bridal departments in several of the stores.

The mall was very upscale and the bridal boutique was not thrilled to have in its by-appointment-only environs a soiled, bloody wedding gown removed from a trash bag.

The manager's attitude changed only slightly when it was determined that the dress had to have come from them because they had an exclusive contract with the designer.

"And then there are times when you just get lucky," Quinn murmured to Cara as the manager went off to check for a record of the purchase.

But this luck didn't extend beyond the initial coincidence. The only thing the manager returned with was a consultant who remembered handling the sale.

"I sold it to a man a few weeks ago. He didn't have an appointment, but he saw the gown in the window and insisted I sell it to him right then. He refused my every attempt to arrange to have his fiancée fitted, even when I offered to go to her. He said he just needed the dress and seemed unconcerned about whether or not his bride would like it or not."

"Did he pay by check or credit card?" Quinn asked the matronly but expensively clad woman.

"He paid in cash," she answered, much nicer than the manager had been and without any airs of superiority. "I remember because he seemed to think flashing hundred-dollar bills at me made up for his lack of courtesy."

"Can you describe him?"

She thought about it. "Your age," she said to Quinn. "Very attractive. Light blond hair, impeccably cut and styled. Dark eyes, not too tall, maybe five foot eight or nine. Trim. And he was wearing a silk suit and Italian shoes, if I don't miss my guess."

"Any distinguishing features? A mole, a scar, a dimple?"

She shook her head. "Nothing I recall. Just an impervious attitude." She looked sideways at the manager and then quietly confided, "We get a lot of that here but he was more than impressed with himself, he was downright rude."

Quinn handed her one of his cards. "If you think of anything else we'd appreciate your letting us know."

He thanked her, stuffed the dress back in the trash bag and they left.

"Well, that told us just enough to be nothing, didn't it?" Cara said on the way to putting the dress in the car.

"It told us we're in the right vicinity. And it was pure luck to hit the store that sold the dress on the first try. That saves us a lot of time."

"But we still don't know anything." Except that her fiancée or new husband carried hundred-dollar bills around, was good-looking and rude, she thought.

"We know more than we did before. You never can tell where one bit of information will lead, or fit in later." Quinn locked the door to his car and they headed back into the mall.

"Seems strange that I didn't buy my own wedding gown," Cara said, though she was glad to know it wasn't her taste that had chosen it. "And that there would be such a rush to have it. Do you think we're talking about a whirlwind romance here?"

"Anything is possible."

Cara wasn't sure why Quinn seemed so noncommittal about it all, as if he didn't want to talk about it. She glanced at him from the corner of her eye as they neared one of the department stores. "You're thinking bad things, aren't you?"

Her exaggeratedly dire tone got a smile out of him. "Right now I'm only thinking of getting you some clothes to wear and a pair of shoes that fit so you stop clopping when you walk,'' he said, holding the door open for her and brooking no more discussion of the matter.

IT WAS LATE by the time they got home and Cara was worn out. They came in from the garage through the back door and she made it as far as one of the kitchen chairs before sinking onto it wearily and leaning her head against the high back.

"We overdid it, didn't we?" Quinn said.

"I'm fine," she lied.

"I can see that. Except for that minor weave in your step and collapsing on that chair, of course."

"What can I say, I'm a dizzy dame."

"Your head hurts again, too, doesn't it?"

"Only a little."

He set her packages on the floor near the doorway and then turned back to her. "How about a nightcap? My grandfather swore by the medicinal qualities of a little warm brandy, lemon and honey to cure whatever ails you. Mostly it just gives you a great night's rest."

"Sounds good, but only if you have one, too. I don't want to drink alone. It could ruin my reputation."

He rounded the island counter to fix the drinks, nodding toward the last newspaper on the table before he went. "Feel up to finishing that while you sit there?"

"Sure," she said, opening it and scanning the first few pages until something else occurred to her. "How come we don't reverse this process and ask the papers to publish my picture with a big Do You Know This Woman? caption? Or call the local TV stations and see if they'll do it?" she asked.

"I don't want to do that except as a last resort."

"Why?"

"You do remember the doctor confirming that you were shot, don't you?"

She did, but somehow it still didn't seem real. At least not real enough to scare her.

Or was it just that she felt so safe and protected with Quinn that it was easy not to dwell on it?

"Cara?" His deep, rich voice called her back from her thoughts.

"Yes, I remember that the doctor agreed with you that I'd been shot," she finally answered.

"Well, to air or publish your picture would let whoever shot you and left you in the mountains know that they failed, that you're all right. It could make you the target for a second attempt."

That made sense.

He brought two mugs of steaming toddy to the table and sat across from her.

"So where do we go from here?" she asked.

"Tomorrow we man the phone lines. We'll go through the phone book and call every wedding chapel and reception hall we can find to see if we can locate the wedding site. Lindsey is coming over to help. I spoke to her while you were getting dressed this afternoon. She's also bringing you more of her clothes to borrow."

That struck a note in Cara, who had spent their entire shopping excursion arguing against Quinn buying her much of anything. And losing the battle in the form of a pair of jeans, two tops, a change of underwear and a pair of tennis shoes. "Why did you insist on buying all this stuff if your sister can just loan me enough to tide me over?" she protested with a nod at the bags on the floor.

He shrugged and took a drink from his mug. "I thought you'd feel better with a few things of your own."

For a moment Cara stared at him, taking him in all over again. He was a big, brawny man's man who could be somewhat brusque and seemed to tolerate no foolishness in anyone. Yet under it all was a tender heart.

Actually, she realized the mixture was evident in his face, a handsome mixture of ruggedness and sensitivity. It was a very appealing combination. And she couldn't help wondering why she hadn't met him before she'd gotten married or engaged to a guy who mistreated nice, elderly saleswomen.

But maybe fate had stepped in, she thought. Maybe whatever had happened to her, had happened before she'd tied the knot and left her in Quinn Strummel's path by design.

Or maybe the brandy was making her whimsical.

"You're a nice person, do you know that?" she said, feeling a sudden well of emotion.

"A prince of a guy," he agreed, smiling for her in a self-mocking way that sluiced into her veins to warm them more than the liquor did.

"I'm serious. You've done more for me than I can ever repay, and you didn't have to. Have I let you know how much I appreciate it?"

"I believe there's been mention of it," he understated. "What you don't know is that I'm just a sucker for ladies with violet eyes. Comes from an early Elizabeth Taylor obsession." He nodded toward her toddy and stood up, leaving his own. "Come on and take that with you. My grandfather claimed it was important to drink it in bed so you can fall right to sleep."

But Cara had begun this and meant to finish it as each sip of the brandy made it seem more important.

"I mean it, Quinn. I'd have been lost without you. Literally," she said as they went to the stairs.

He waited for her at the foot of them, and when she headed up he followed, keeping just one hand splayed against the middle of her back for support. His touch ignited the alcohol in her bloodstream and she knew a sudden fierce urge to feel that hand on other parts of her body.

But she tried to ignore it.

"I want you to keep a record of everything it costs to have me around—what you spent today, and your usual fee for investigating," she said as they walked past his room to hers.

His hand was still on her back but he gave no indication he was paying any attention to what she was saying. When they reached the door to her room she turned to face him, rolling within the wall of his arm and ending up much closer to him than she'd had any intention of being.

He put his hand on the doorjamb behind her and stared down at her. "Careful what you're signing on for. This could be a big payback."

She couldn't tell if there was innuendo in that or not. "It's worth it," she answered, though somehow a breathy quality had come into her own voice from just looking into his eyes. "I don't know if I'm rich or poor or somewhere in-between, but even if I can't afford to pay you in money, I could come and answer your phone," she persisted, trying to keep in mind that she really had been talking business. But even so she couldn't resist adding with a grin, "Or help you solve other cases."

That made him laugh, a delightful sound there in the closeness of the hallway. But as if it had released something more between them, the air changed. It suddenly seemed charged with electricity.

Or was it just the liquor?

If it was, she thought, then Quinn was similarly influenced because there he was, staring down at her instead of saying good-night, holding her with his eyes.

His expression sobered in slow degrees and he seemed almost troubled by something. "Let's not play with fire, Cara," he said in a gravelly voice.

She could have asked what he meant since they'd really only been talking about her paying for his services as a P.I. But she knew very well that there was more going on beneath the surface.

She ordered herself to tell him he was right, that they shouldn't play with fire. Or at least to nod her agreement. But instead she just met the heat of his gaze and watched it do a slow descent to her mouth as her head fell a little farther back all on its own and her lips parted.

"Dammit," he muttered so softly she barely heard him before his free hand slid to the side of her neck, just where it had been the night before, though this time it was almost as if something dragged it there against his will.

The same something that made her tilt her head against his hand, curling into his caress even as she knew she shouldn't.

She saw a muscle tense in his jaw, yet his lips opened in the same way hers had a moment before, only slightly, almost as if just to breathe.

Then, so slowly he barely moved, his mouth captured hers in a kiss that was tentative, soft, sweet. So sweet it made her ache for more, for him to release some of the power held in check in that big body of his, to pull her against him, to meld her to him.

But that didn't happen.

In fact, it was a kiss that seemed as if it could end at any moment, as if he knew it should. Just the way she did.

It didn't, though. Instead he deepened it, parting his lips over hers, inviting her to do the same, to taste the fruit they both knew might be forbidden.

And then, finally, common sense won out and Quinn nearly tore away from her.

Cara opened her eyes to the liquid silver of his feasting on her with a hunger that denied that ending, letting her know that he, too, wanted to be doing much, much more.

"See, I'm no prince," he said in a voice ragged with restraint.

Cara didn't say anything. But he was right. He was much better. She poked a finger to his chest, doing her part to break the spell that had woven them together. "Prove it by running a tab on what I owe you," she challenged.

He only raised his chin over her head toward her room. "Get in there and go to bed before I have to take you to the hospital for brandy-induced delirium," he ordered.

Then he turned her by the shoulders, pushed her gently inside and closed the door firmly between them.

But he was wrong if he thought the liquor had had anything to do with that kiss, because it hadn't.

Any more than it was responsible for her going to bed wishing for the warmth of more than his hot toddy.

For it was Quinn himself who inspired it all. And her attraction to him was something much headier than any brandy.

Chapter Four

Quinn turned off the hot water, turned up the cold full blast, braced both palms against the wall on either side of the shower head and eased himself into the frigid spray.

It was a rude awakening.

One he needed after a night filled with more self-castigation than sleep. With more fantasizing and wanting and fighting the urge to go into the room next to his for a second round of the kissing that shouldn't have been in the first place.

But this morning he had a plan. He intended to do everything he could not to be alone with Cara.

He had already arranged for Lindsey to come in today to help call wedding chapels and the like. He would persuade her to stay for dinner and on into the evening. And he'd get Logan to join them, too.

There was safety in numbers. Having other people around would keep him from giving in to the attraction that had overpowered him the night before. It would keep him from kissing Cara again—from doing more than kissing her, no matter how much he wanted to.

And he definitely wanted to. Big time.

Somehow, in a way no one had ever managed so quickly, she'd reached a spot in him that not many people could at all.

Being a cop and a P.I. had taught him to have a rigid control over his feelings. It was a matter of survival. Either job was impossible if the things he saw or heard, the people he met, could get to him on a personal or emotional level. But to go from keeping that distance to letting other people get close was tough.

Sure he had soft spots for his family. Hell, thinking about Lindsey being in Cara's situation was what had gotten Cara in his house in the first place. But beyond his folks, or Logan or Lindsey, there were few people—even women—who could penetrate that barrier to touch him inside. Damn few.

But for some reason he didn't understand, Cara was one of them. More than one of them, she'd dug in deeper and more effortlessly than any woman he'd ever met.

Why? he asked himself as even the cold water didn't make him not want her.

She was different, he thought as he analyzed. She was a little nutty. She had a lighthearted perspective that was very appealing. She didn't overdramatize or take herself or anything else too seriously. She was fun. And funny. And she did what few outside of his family had ever been able to do—she brought out his lighter side.

That was an accomplishment. Because along with burying the sensitive, vulnerable parts of him, there had emerged a seriousness that wasn't easily breached, either. A seriousness that felt good to shed when he could.

Of course it didn't hurt that she was great looking. And sexy.

Put it all together and he was as helpless as a damn kitten in resisting her.

The trouble was, she was also not just a single, unencumbered woman he'd met on the street or in line at the grocery store or on a blind date. And he knew he should be fighting like hell to find a way to put that old professional distance between them, to resist the attraction and everything she stirred in him.

But he was having trouble mustering that fight.

So he'd bring in his sister and brother to run interference. To keep things between himself and Cara on a level surface.

To keep his hands off her.

And his lips.

And his thoughts.

But that last part was futile, he knew. Because she was there in his mind from the minute he woke up in the morning until he forced himself from fantasies of her to sleep at night.

And nothing and nobody seemed to be able to change that.

THIS MORNING CARA KNEW it was no dizzy spell when she first looked into the mirror and had the reaction that was like being momentarily blinded by a camera flash.

She felt one hundred percent fine. Her head didn't hurt at all, nor was it spinning sickeningly as it had the day before.

But her heart was pounding and adrenaline poured into her veins with the rush of fear that hit her the moment she glanced into that mirror.

No memory came with it, no opening of the locked door in her mind. Just an overwhelming sense of danger that sent her hurrying to put on her new jeans and a red camp shirt and get downstairs to Quinn.

He was making pancakes for breakfast and stopped midflip when she came into the kitchen, to frown at her. "You look like somebody's chasing you."

"Demons," she told him, only half joking.

He made a show of looking behind her. "I don't see any."

She pointed to her head. "They're in here."

His eyebrows rose in surprise. "Is your memory back?"

"No, it's just that the strangest thing happens to me when I look in the mirror." She went on to explain as best she could something that was so ambiguous, so hard even for her to grasp.

"Déjà vu?" he asked when she finished.

"Yes, sort of like that. Like I'm reliving something but I don't know what. I just can't understand why the sight of my own face would cause it. I mean, it's one thing not to remember what I look like so that it's as if I'm seeing someone who seems sort of familiar but not in any concrete way. But why would it cause almost a blackout and leave me feeling like I should run away to save myself? It's my own face, for crying out loud."

"It could just be shock, Cara. It can play tricks on the mind. Or it could be coming from the head injury. Maybe the light over the mirror hits just right and blinds you for a moment—like the vision disturbances of a migraine—and it scares you because so many things are off kilter now."

But those explanations seemed so mundane. She thought of a better one. "Or maybe I have an identical twin sister and that's who shot me, so when I see my own face I'm also seeing the face of the person who did this to me."

His mouth eased into a smile that looked as if it wanted to be a laugh. "Or maybe you have one of the world's greatest imaginations."

"That, too," she conceded because the twin theory did sound more like a TV movie than anything that was likely to have happened. Though how could she tell what was likely to have happened in a situation as unlikely as this one?

"As I said before, anything is possible," he added, not patronizing her, but also clearly not buying the twin scenario. "Between the head wound, amnesia and some inevitable shock, everything that flits through your mind could mean nothing as easily as it could mean something. But don't let it scare you."

Nothing frightened her when she was with him, but she didn't say that. Instead she said, "Who, me?" as if he'd only imagined she'd come scurrying down to him.

But Cara had the sense that her fear wasn't the only feeling being denied in that kitchen at that moment.

Quinn seemed to be keeping some distance between them, stepping away when she came within a few feet of him, watching his pancakes cook rather than looking at her, never letting his eyes linger when his gaze did touch her.

It was for the best, she knew. That kiss the night before had been a mistake. Wonderful, but a mistake. They both needed to back off, and if disappointment was another of those misplaced feelings in the room with them, it was also another one she needed to deny.

Because they had no business getting romantically involved with each other.

So Cara aided what he'd begun and put some space of her own between them.

Over breakfast they discussed her improved health, and this time, when she offered to help clean up, he accepted.

By the time they'd finished, his sister arrived.

Lindsey Strummel. She'd taken back her maiden name after her divorce, Quinn explained during his introduction.

She was Cara's height and had Quinn's same coloring, though there was otherwise little resemblance between sister and brother. Lindsey's face was elegant, with high, prominent cheekbones, a slender nose, wide eyes the same sparkling silver and skin like alabaster. Her dark brown hair was shot through with coppery streaks, and she wore it short and simply cut in a waifish style, with the top left slightly long and the sides and back close cropped.

And although Quinn had said she was emotionally fragile since the recent end of her marriage, she didn't show it. She greeted Cara with a warmth that made her seem like a friend.

"You don't look like a private investigator," Cara informed her when the amenities were taken care of. "I expected someone mannish and intimidating."

"To deal with car chases, shootouts, pistol whippings, fistfights and all the rest of what she imagines being a P.I. involves," Quinn said over her shoulder with a wink in his voice.

"I can be pretty intimidating when I need to be," Lindsey assured. "But I don't usually need to be. Most people respond better to friendliness or tact. In fact, sometimes I can get more cooperation than Quinn just because I'm not so stern and imposing.''

"But when a tough guy is needed, I'm on the job,'' he said like a bad commercial.

"Don't let him fool you,'' Lindsey added in an aside to Cara. "He's really a great big teddy bear.''

Cara glanced at him to see his reaction to that, trying to ignore the little skip her heart gave at the thought of how nice it would be to curl up in that big teddy bear's embrace.

"Are we going to stand around here all day wasting time discussing me?'' he asked then. "Or can we get some work done?''

"He's modest, too. That tone means we're embarrassing him,'' Lindsey tutored on the way to getting down to business.

CARA USED the private telephone line, Quinn used Strummel Investigations' business line and Lindsey went out to the carriage house to use Logan's phone. Between the three of them they called every church, chapel, temple, wedding consultant, reception hall, bridal shop and registry in the phone book. By that evening they'd all come up with exactly the same result—nothing.

"The wedding that wasn't?'' Cara asked as they regrouped in Quinn's living room.

"Not necessarily. It could have been held in a private home without a lot of fuss or formality,'' Quinn offered.

"Just with a two-thousand-dollar wedding dress,'' Cara commented on what seemed incongruous in that theory.

"There could have been some premeditation involved. If it was a wedding scam, the groom wouldn't want to leave any kind of trail that would lead to him later," Lindsey noted.

Cara caught Quinn shaking his head at his sister as if to warn her not to say any more in that vein.

So he did suspect the worst of Peter Whos-its, but he was trying to protect her from it. "It's all right," she told him. "If my fiancé or groom did this I'm going to find out sooner or later, anyway."

"But we don't need to point a finger at anyone until we have something more than supposition to go on."

"Supposition and a poorly treated saleslady," Cara added because it troubled her. Sure Peter Whos-its could have just been having a bad day or been in a rush, but it was difficult to like the image of a man who treated people shabbily. And what about the fact that he bought her a wedding gown without any consideration of her taste, without so much as consulting her, without even caring if it fit?

She couldn't feel heartened by the fact that he'd apparently had no more regard for her in that respect than he'd had for the saleswoman's feelings. And if he hadn't had any regard for her in that respect, did he have any in any other respect?

"I say we call it a day on this subject," Quinn suggested. "Logan should be here anytime and—"

As if on cue, Logan came in just then, overloaded with a wine bottle, cartons of Chinese food and two video-cassette tapes of movies he'd rented.

"Perfect timing," Lindsey said as she went to help her brother.

Quinn brought paper plates, napkins, silverware and glasses from the kitchen and the four of them settled around the coffee table.

"Anything turn up today?" Logan asked as they passed around the cartons of sesame chicken, twice-cooked pork, pepper steak and chow mein.

"Zilch," Quinn answered. "Did you hear anything from Jackson at the DMV?"

"Only that he's staying late tonight to work on the search. I gave him this number in case he comes up with anything."

"No stray grooms turned up, either, I assume?"

"Sorry," Logan said to Cara even though he was answering Quinn's question.

"I thought we were finished talking about this for the day?" Lindsey reminded.

"We are," Quinn said with finality. Then he held up a forkful of chow mein. "We're just going to enjoy eating worms."

Cara stopped her own fork in midair.

Lindsey rolled her eyes and explained to her, "I'm the youngest. And the only girl. That means my two delightful older brothers tortured me as a kid. The first time I had Chinese food they told me horrible things about it being made of worms and spiders' legs, and worse. So of course I wouldn't eat it and they got it all to themselves. I have since learned to ignore them," she finished with a flourish that put a large helping of chow mein in her mouth.

"How far apart are all of you?" Cara asked when she'd managed a bite of her own.

"There are two years between Quinn and Logan, but only a year between Logan and me," Lindsey answered. "I'm the baby at thirty-four."

"The *big* baby," Logan goaded.

"He's thirty-five," Lindsey answered back. "And Quinn is a whopping thirty-seven. You know what that means—"

"Means he's the closest to forty," Logan interjected to jab Quinn, too.

"It means I'm older and wiser," Quinn said.

"And they treated you badly as kids?" Cara asked Lindsey, getting into the spirit of their camaraderie.

"Horrible."

"She deserved it," Logan informed.

"She was no saint," Quinn confirmed.

"I was, too," Lindsey countered, though there was too much audacity in her voice to believe her.

"Who was it who brought pictures of Christmas morning to school and told all my friends I got a doll when all I was doing was looking at yours?" Logan accused.

"And who was it who collected a quarter from half a dozen girls and sneaked them into the bathroom while I was showering?" Quinn added.

"You both deserved it—you locked me in a closet for three hours."

"Because you wouldn't leave us alone to impress the new girls up the block."

"And we gave you pretzels," Quinn said, as if she were being ungrateful.

"Oh, big deal—pretzels. Who used to hold me down and make me lick the carpet whenever I did something you didn't like?"

"Lick the carpet?" Cara repeated in amused disgust.

"She developed quite a taste for it," Quinn said.

Affronted, Lindsey went on. "And who dropped me off the balcony of our hotel room when we went to Colorado Springs that summer on vacation?"

"There was a swimming pool right underneath," Logan defended.

"And I was twelve and in my nightgown, which was completely transparent when wet."

"So she shaved off my eyebrows while I slept and I started eleventh grade that way," Quinn said.

"And she used black permanent marker on all my fingernails. I went to school looking like a freak, too," Logan added.

"Herb Newton," Lindsey countered, her voice soaked in mock malice.

Both Quinn and Logan burst out laughing. "That one was rotten," Quinn agreed.

By then Cara had finished eating and just sat with her back against the sofa, enjoying them. "Who was Herb Newton?"

"Not who. What," Lindsey amended. "They had the most gorgeous hunk of upperclassman introduce himself to me as Herb Newton and ask me to the homecoming dance when I was a freshman. I was new to the school and so was he. How could I have guessed these two jerks had already enlisted him? Of course I accepted."

"Accepted?" Logan cut in. "You nearly fell at his feet. And then you gloated and went around saying he was so much better than your pond-scum brothers."

"I was all ready to go. The doorbell rang. And out on the porch was a goat with a bow tie around its neck and a name tag that said Herb Newton."

"Oh, that's mean!" Cara judged.

"See, I told you," Lindsey said victoriously.

"Don't worry," Logan put in, "None of us got to go to the dance. Quinn's and my dates hated us. And the next week Lindsey cut both our hair in our sleep—big, gaping chunks right down to the scalp in some places. We looked like we'd gone to a samurai barber, and it took six months to grow out."

"Even Logan couldn't get a date then," Quinn said with a laugh.

"You guys were all terrible," Cara decreed as they picked up the mess and went to the kitchen to make popcorn to go with their movies.

"Spark any images of brothers and sisters of your own, by any chance?" Quinn asked on the way, bending low to her ear.

It was the closest he'd been to her all day and evening, and the warmth of his breath against her skin was enough to make her pulse kick up a notch. "I'm wondering if I want to remember brothers or sisters like you guys," she joked.

But she didn't mean it. In spite of all the three Strummels had inflicted on one another as kids, it was clear how close they were now. If one of them were suddenly to disappear, she knew the other two wouldn't rest until the missing one were found. And she recognized in herself just a little envy of their funny memories and the sense of unquestioned membership in a private club.

But she was also grateful to be included and counted her blessings all over again that it was Quinn who had found her in the meadow.

"Just put a *little* of the jalapeño pepper I like in my popcorn," Lindsey warned Quinn as she and Logan went back to the living room to set up for the movies.

"Last time you were too heavy-handed and you gave me heartburn."

"Complaints. All I get are complaints. You're not too big for me to make you lick the carpet, you know," he called back. Then, when he and Cara were alone, he muttered, "She gets a double dose now."

Cara laughed at him.

"What're you laughing at?" he demanded in mock aggravation as he popped the corn.

"You. You've been so upstanding and respectable and conscientious and mature since we met, I didn't know there was this ornery side to you."

His handsome face eased into a slow grin. "Me? Ornery? Never."

"Are you guys like this all the time?"

"No, sometimes we're a lot worse."

"You must have driven your folks crazy."

"We did. But they're the kind of people who genuinely like kids, so they weren't too hard on us. I think we sort of entertained them." He nodded over his shoulder. "There's bowls in that cupboard. Would you get four of them, please?"

Cara did, bringing them to the island counter. He removed the pan from the heat and set it on a cool burner while he melted butter in the microwave. When he'd salted and buttered the whole batch he divided it among the bowls, but only one did he douse liberally in jalapeño-pepper powder.

Cara watched him, enjoying the sight of him as a great big mischievous kid.

He raised a conspiratorial smile to her. "This'll be our secret."

"And if I don't keep it?" she threatened, teasing him.

"I'll sneak in while you sleep and do something evil to you. Don't forget that's the Strummels' favorite time to strike."

But Cara knew better than to believe he could do anything evil. Deliciously wicked, maybe, but not evil.

And the thought of him coming into her room for that was much too tempting.

She picked up two of the bowls and headed out of the kitchen then. "Come on," she said as she bumped the swinging door open with her hip. "I'll pretend I didn't see." Just as she was pretending she wasn't thinking about what those broad shoulders of his might look like bare, awash in moonlight filtering in through her window during a night raid on her bedroom.

By the time Cara and Quinn got back to the living room, Lindsey and Logan had usurped the two armchairs. That left only the couch for Cara and Quinn to share.

Situated the way the furniture was, the television could be seen from one end of the sofa, but not from the other, which put them both at the TV-friendly end. Cara hugged the armrest and Quinn seemed to keep as much distance as he could.

Until his sister tasted her popcorn, discovered it was too hot to eat and stole his bowl.

"Next time I'll put my own pepper in it," she said.

"You can't have all of mine. Just mix some of it into yours so the pepper isn't so concentrated," he argued.

"I don't want any of it with pepper now," she said, her nose in the air. "You'll just have to go without."

"You can share mine," Cara said, with nothing on her mind other than popcorn. But the offer brought Quinn nearer to her on the couch. And when he'd finished making himself comfortable by propping his feet on the coffee table and stretching his arms along the sofa back, she was effectively surrounded by him.

Then Logan started the movie and turned off all the lights.

There was nothing for Cara to do but relax in the warm shell of Quinn's side. But being that close to him made it difficult not to wish his arm would slip off the back of the couch to her shoulders. Not to picture herself leaning into him, laying her head against his chest, maybe entwining her legs with those long, muscular ones of his.

Sitting there in the dark with him, breathing in the scent of his after-shave, it was virtually impossible not to imagine what it would feel like to have him press a kiss to the top of her head or tip her face up to him and have him cover her mouth with his in the way he had the night before. Only more than the night before—in a deeper kiss with mouths open and tongues playing.

Maybe he would hold her so tightly she'd hardly be able to move. Or he might pull her up onto his lap and she'd feel the rise of him as she buried her hands in his hair and found out if it was really as silky as it looked. Maybe one of those big, capable hands would find her breast and—

"Are you okay?" Quinn whispered, jolting her back to reality.

"Sure. Why?" she answered too quickly.

"You're breathing hard. Maybe this shoot-'em-up movie wasn't a good choice."

Cara could feel heat suffusing her face and thanked God the lights were off so he couldn't see what felt like a monumental blush. "No, no, I'm fine. The movie's fine," she assured, though in truth she hadn't really seen a minute of it.

He seemed to accept that and again turned his attention to the television.

Cara took a deep breath and let it out in a carefully silent sigh as she fought any lingering effects of the daydream. It didn't help that he was still so close beside her that if either of them moved even slightly their thighs brushed. Or that she had such an intense awareness of him that even something as simple as that could make her every nerve ending stand up and take notice.

She just had to not think about him, she told herself.

Or at least she had to try.

She stared at the TV screen with a new intensity. She ate popcorn. She even joined in when everybody commented on the movie.

But it was all superficial.

Underneath, every sense was homed in on Quinn.

IT WAS NEARLY MIDNIGHT by the time both of the movies Logan had rented were over. Good-nights were being said all around when the phone rang.

"That could be Jackson," Logan reminded.

"Come and answer it," Quinn suggested, bringing his brother in from the laundry room, where Logan and Lindsey had been about to leave.

Lindsey wandered back, too, just as Logan nodded to them all to let them know the caller was indeed Jackson from the Department of Motor Vehicles.

Logan took a pencil and tablet from a drawer nearby and wrote what was apparently being said on the other end. Then he thanked his caller, said he'd buy him a beer next time he saw him and hung up.

"Pay dirt," he told his audience. "Your name is Cara Elizabeth Walsh and your address is an apartment in Arvada."

"Cara Walsh," she repeated, trying it out. When it didn't strike a chord she shrugged obliquely. "Okay. Where's Arvada?"

"It's a suburb west of here. Not far," Quinn offered.

Logan handed Quinn the paper and took Lindsey's arm, heading for the door again. "Our work here is done, Tonto. Let's head for the hills."

The good-nights were repeated, and they left.

"Well," Cara said when she and Quinn were alone. "Should you take me home?"

He chuckled. "Just like that? No, I don't think so. But we could drive by if you want, let you take a look at the place, see if it nudges your memory."

Yes, they could do that. But did she want to? "It's awfully late," she hedged.

"It's only about a twenty-minute drive from here," he said, taking his car keys off the countertop and heading for the back door.

But Cara didn't follow him. Instead she stayed rooted to the kitchen floor. Her stomach was jumping something fierce, and she was suddenly very unnerved by the prospect of leaping back into her own life.

Belatedly Quinn realized he was the only one on his way out. From the laundry room he said, "We don't have to go if you don't want to."

That was the point. She didn't know if she wanted to or not.

"Cara?" he said when she didn't answer and didn't budge, either.

She reminded herself that they were only going to drive by. That it wasn't as if he would leave her on the doorstep. And she was curious. Though in a removed sort of way, as if they'd be looking at the apartment of someone she didn't know.

"Maybe this wasn't a good idea," Quinn said, stepping back into the doorway between the kitchen and the laundry room.

"No, it's okay. Let's go," she said with enough enthusiasm to make it almost real, finally putting one foot in front of the other to follow him out to the garage.

"Cara Walsh," she said again once they were in Quinn's car and headed for the highway.

"How does it feel to you?"

She shrugged. "It's just a name."

"Not quite. It's *your* name. Fingerprints don't lie."

"Oh, I wasn't doubting it. It's just that it doesn't seem to mean anything to me." Then something else occurred to her. "I forgot to thank Logan for his trouble."

"He probably didn't even notice. All in the line of duty—sort of."

"So this is detective work?" she said, thinking about how easily her identity had been discovered. "Just a couple of fingerprints sent to the driver's license bureau and the case is closed. No deep delving. No careful piecing together of the puzzle. No thrill-a-minute action and adventure. Very disappointing."

He smiled over at her in the dim light of the car interior. "Isn't it though? And here I was wanting to dazzle you."

He'd dazzled her, but it didn't have anything to do with his work.

"But who says the case is closed?" he asked then.

"It isn't?"

"We know your name and address but we still don't know who shot you or why. We can hardly just ignore that."

Cara perked up. "That's true. Like you said before, they could try again."

He laughed. "Don't sound so happy about it."

She tried to curb her excitement. Not that the prospect of someone taking a shot at her excited her, but the idea of more time with Quinn did.

"You ought to be looking around. We're getting close," he said.

She focused on what they were passing, seeing quiet suburban streets now that they'd left the highway and followed a main road over a hill to curve into a valley on the other side.

There wasn't much to distinguish Arvada. A grocery store. A discount house. A senior citizens' high rise. A bowling alley. A shoppette. A gas station.

Small brick homes lined the streets that Quinn turned onto, all of them the same ranch style, most of them with well-tended yards and trees that were not quite as tall as those in Quinn's neighborhood.

The apartment building at the address Logan's friend had given them was on a cul-de-sac amid the homes. It was three stories of burnished red brick, balconies and security doors at each of six different sections that made access impossible without a key.

Quinn backed into one of the few empty spots in the parking lot and turned off the engine.

Most of the apartment's windows were dark, including those of the one designated as the manager's.

Cara was glad they couldn't go there tonight and ask to be let into the place the DMV had registered as hers.

Quinn didn't say anything. She assumed he was letting her soak up everything in view to allow it a full chance to raise a memory. It didn't. Not anything beyond the same vague sense of familiarity she had about her own face.

So this is where I live, she thought. "I wonder if I share the place with Peter Whos-its?" she heard herself say the moment it occurred to her that she might.

"I'll find out," Quinn offered, getting out of the car.

A sudden wave of panic rushed through Cara, but her, "No, that's okay," was lost to the door closing behind him. Instead she was left watching as he began to check names on the mailboxes in the lighted doorways that led to each section of the building.

What if he found her apartment and Peter Whos-its's name was on the mailbox along with hers? What if Quinn rang the bell to the apartment and found him home?

God, she didn't want that to happen! Not yet. Not right now. She wasn't ready!

The force of her feelings gave her pause.

Shouldn't she be thrilled to find out who she was, where she lived, to get back what she'd lost to a blank memory?

Maybe she should be, but she wasn't.

If she had to have amnesia, it was easier to have it in a situation involving people to whom she was a stranger, she decided. The idea of being where she belonged, with people she should know but didn't, was somehow more disconcerting. There would be expectations of her that she might not be able to fulfill. Memories she was supposed to have but couldn't dredge up. Duties and jobs she needed to do that she didn't have a clue how to perform.

But the amnesia wasn't the only reason she wasn't anxious to be back in her own life, she realized as she watched those long legs of Quinn's take him from one security door to the next.

There was Quinn, too....

Then she saw him straighten from his study of names on the mailboxes in the farthest doorway down and push one of the buttons on the panel.

Her stomach did a flip-flop.

She listened for an answering buzz that would open the door, unsure if she'd be able to hear it over the thunderous pounding of her heart.

But no buzz sounded and after a moment Quinn just came back to the car.

"Cara Walsh, apartment 33C," he announced.

"And?"

"And that's it. Only your name on the mailbox. And no answer when I rang the bell for that apartment."

She breathed a sigh of relief.

"Are you okay? You're on the edge of your seat."

She hadn't realized it. Or that she was hanging on to the dashboard with a white-knuckled grip. She let go and sat back. "Sure. I'm fine."

His sidelong glance at her was dubious but he didn't say anything about it. "Is being here doing anything for your memory?"

"Not a thing."

"Want to stay a little longer or just come back tomorrow?"

"We can go home." Funny, but that's what his house felt like to her—home—while this place that really was home didn't raise that feeling at all. Crazy. Maybe she really had gone crazy.

Quinn started the engine and pulled out of the parking lot, heading back the way they'd come.

The farther they got from the place, the more Cara relaxed. But something about what felt like a close call in contacting Peter Whos-its made her begin to think about women in Quinn's life. Since meeting him she'd felt she had him all to herself, but now that seemed unrealistic.

"Do you have a girlfriend?" she asked out of the blue.

He laughed and glanced over at her as if she'd lost her mind. "Where did that come from?"

"I was just wondering."

His eyebrows pulsed into a frown that didn't stay longer than a second. "No, I don't know anyone I'd call a girlfriend."

"But you do date?"

"Sure."

"Have you ever been married?"

"Only once but that was in the fifth grade for a home science project. And it didn't last. Our five-pound sack-of-flour baby got torn open during an impromptu football game that cast the baby as the ball. Put an end to the marriage."

"And you haven't even been tempted since then?"

"Not really." He hesitated, but she had the sense he was debating about saying more so she waited. Finally he added, "Women tell me I'm hard to get close to."

"They do? I haven't found that to be true."

He didn't say anything to that.

"So it's Strummel Investigations and Monastery," she joked, liking the idea so much it raised her spirits back to where they'd been before the call from Logan's friend at the DMV.

"Monastery?" Quinn laughed out loud as he eased off the highway. "Not quite. I can't lay claim to being a monk."

"Oh, now I'm jealous," she said as if she were still kidding when in fact she didn't like the thought of him with other women at all, not even in the past tense.

"How do you think I feel about old Peter Whosits?" he countered.

That pleased her no end. "Well, at least I only have one. And I can't even remember him. And you think he shot me. That's easier to handle than legions of adoring lovelies."

"Legions of adoring lovelies," he repeated, seeming to try it on for size. Then, as if he liked the fit, "Absolutely. Legions. A different woman for every day of the year," he kidded, turning onto his street.

"Ah, then I've been cramping your style. You're three behind by now."

He pulled into the drive and then into the garage. "That's all right. I can hold them over for next year."

"Good, now I don't have to feel guilty."

He leaned over to her ear and said, "Feel your oats, feel the wind in your hair, feel my muscles, but never feel guilty."

Forget the oats and the wind in her hair, but the muscles were a different story. Her hands were itching to feel those. But he was oblivious to it, getting out of the car and waiting for her at the garage entrance.

Cara drew a short, shallow breath, blew it out and joined him with her hands jammed safely into her pockets.

Quinn held open the back door to the house and once they were both in, locked it after them. In the kitchen he tossed his keys on the counter where they'd been before. "Better get some rest. Tomorrow could be a big day."

Their silly banter had pushed away thoughts of the progress they'd made on her case tonight, but now they came back, complete with the tension.

Cara didn't want it to show so she merely went along with him through the dark house and up the stairs.

"We'll go back to the apartment in the morning," he said along the way. "Meet the manager, see what he knows about you, get him to let us into your place and take it from there."

But to where?

They'd reached Quinn's bedroom door by then, and she had only to peer at the next one to know she wasn't going to be able to sleep. "On second thought, I'm not really tired. I think I'll go down and watch some television."

He leaned a shoulder against the wall and pinned her in place with a curious frown. "Are you nervous? Excited? Scared?"

She shrugged. "Let's just say I'm having some mixed up feelings about...things."

"Things?"

Him. Going back to her real life. Everything. "I told you I was kind of enjoying the freedom of a clear slate."

He nodded his understanding. "It's only natural that you'd be uneasy. After all, someone in your past did you harm. But it'll be okay. I won't let anything happen to you."

"Even if my whole life opens up tomorrow, you won't leave me alone with it?" she tested.

"Even then." There was suddenly a husky timbre to his voice, and the air between them went from teasing to something more. To something close and intimate.

Cara looked into his silver eyes and thought there was no way a saleswoman abuser was going to stand up to him. "Or we could just skip finding me," she heard herself suggest, only partly joking again.

He gave her one of those slow smiles. "What if you're the heir to the throne of Nova Scotia and world peace depends on you? Or you do some vitally important research that will save millions of lives but no one else can finish it?" he proposed, clearly letting his imagination devise scenarios the way she usually did.

But this time Cara's imagination didn't take flight. She was too firmly rooted in the present. In Quinn. "What if I'm a nine-to-fiver? An ordinary person who leads an ordinary life that no one has missed me dropping out of? What if I'm just plain and boring and it wouldn't matter if I never went back?"

"That's not you," he said very quietly and without having to consider it. "Even if you are an ordinary person leading an ordinary life, I know for a fact that you aren't plain or boring."

He reached out and stroked her cheek with just the backs of his fingers then, and she couldn't help leaning into that caress just a little, absorbing the feel of that gentle touch, the texture of his skin.

It was agony to want so much more and know she was out of line. To know she couldn't have more. To know that at this time tomorrow night she could be in a different place, with a different man. A man she just didn't believe in her heart was all this man was.

And at that moment she wanted only to stay forever with Quinn stroking her cheek, bathed in the molten silver of his gaze as he smiled that smile that crinkled the corners of his eyes and drew parentheses on either side of his mouth. A mouth she wanted badly to feel on hers.

She covered his hand with her own, and that was all it took for him to lay his palm along the side of her face.

This hallway was getting to be a dangerous place, she thought, remembering the kiss they'd shared there the night before. But she was willing to dance with a little danger.

She raised her eyes to him again, willing him to kiss her. Ready for it. Dying for it.

His gaze locked onto hers, held it. His lips parted just slightly. He leaned nearer and she tilted her chin...

But then his jaw tensed, he pulled away, hand and all, and swallowed so hard she saw his Adam's apple rise and fall.

"We better see what tomorrow brings," he said in a tight, ragged voice.

Of course he was right. And she knew it. But that didn't take away the disappointment. Or the lingering yearning for his kiss, his arms around her...

How could tomorrow bring anything better than that?

But Cara took a deep breath that straightened her shoulders and turned toward the stairs. "Tomorrow," she said like a soldier charging a foe.

For that's what it felt like to her.

But she didn't feel as steadfast as she sounded, and she couldn't help one last glance at Quinn over her shoulder as she descended the first step.

He was still standing there, watching her go, his expression as tense as she felt in response to every unsatiated urge that was roiling around inside of her.

"Want to watch TV with me?" she invited, as if what was between them wasn't hot enough to turn the hallway into a sauna.

"If I went downstairs with you I wouldn't see any more of whatever is on television than I saw of either of those movies tonight. Only there wouldn't be company to keep me an honorable man."

What did that mean? That he'd been as secretly preoccupied with her all night as she'd been with him? It delighted her to think so. It tantalized and teased her. But nothing was going to come of it. And it was for the best.

"Good night, then," she forced herself to say, going down the rest of the stairs.

And wondering all the way why what was best felt so bad.

Chapter Five

"Hey, lady, are you going to sleep all day?"

The deep masculine voice rolled over her like slow-running honey, making Cara want to snuggle even deeper into her sleep. She settled for snuggling deeper into the couch cushions and opening her eyes to the glorious first sight of Quinn sitting on the coffee table.

His white shirtsleeves were turned back to elbows that were braced on jean-clad thighs spread wide so a steaming mug could be held between them, not far from her face.

"Morning," she said sleepily.

"Actually, it's nearly noon."

Was she a chronic late sleeper, she wondered, or were recent circumstances the cause? She sat up, realizing only then that she'd acquired a blanket at some point. "Where did this come from?"

"I came down about three-thirty, saw you'd fallen asleep and covered you."

Nice man, even if he did say that a little gruffly. "Thanks. But what were you doing down here at that time of the night?"

"Insomnia," he answered somewhat under his breath, as if he didn't want to admit it.

"I must have just fallen asleep. The last time I looked at the clock it was 3:10."

He held the mug out to her. "Tea. Strong and caffeinated."

"Thanks." She accepted the cup and took a careful sip. "Did you get any sleep at all?"

He nodded to one of the overstuffed chairs, where another blanket was flung over the back. "After a while."

She made a face. "You mean you watched me sleep?"

"A little."

She groaned. "Why didn't you just kick me and tell me to go to bed?"

"And leave myself alone with nothing but the 'Home Shopping Club'?" he asked wryly. "Besides, I was taught never to kick a woman."

"I hope I don't snore or drool or give away state secrets or do something too awful in my sleep."

"You don't. You hardly breathe and you don't move a muscle. But you ought to now so we can get going."

To the apartment. She'd forgotten about it.

"I've already showered."

He didn't have to tell her that—he looked fresh and clean shaven and he smelled like the woods on a spring day.

"Why don't you go on up and get ready while I fix us an omelet," he suggested, "and then we'll see if we can't accomplish something yet today."

She was in no hurry. "I thought you couldn't trust yourself to come down here with me last night?" she said instead, curious as to why he had.

"I couldn't," he answered flatly.

"But you did. Later."

He stood and folded his blanket. But he didn't answer her.

"Did you have dishonorable intentions?" she persisted, trying to sound as if she were kidding.

"Let's just say it was good that you were asleep," he murmured almost inaudibly and certainly with no humor.

"What if I hadn't been?" Would she have been playing with fire the way she sensed she was at that moment?

He leveled those silver eyes on her. "If you hadn't been I'd have done something I'd probably be regretting right now," he said more sternly than she'd ever heard him.

He took a deep breath, stared at the ceiling for a moment and then frowned at her again. "Look, there's no denying that I'm attracted to you, Cara. Drawn to you, turned on by you—the whole nine yards. And there's also no denying that in my entire damn life I've never had it this bad. But we don't know who the hell you are, beyond a name and address. We don't know if you're married. We don't know if you're madly in love with somebody. All we do know is that there's a chance of both of those things or you wouldn't have been in that expensive wedding gown in the first place. Now, I don't know how you read that, but to me it means hands-off. So whether or not it's obvious, I'm trying to keep my damn hands off," he finished, each of those last words spoken with deliberate intensity through clenched teeth.

"I'm sorry," she said, feeling bad for pushing him and making light of the kind of self-control she should be practicing right along with him. "I guess I'm just nervous about today and I wasn't thinking. But you're absolutely right."

He sighed, shook his head and raked a hand through his hair. "No, I'm sorry," he added, sounding genuinely contrite. "I shouldn't have snapped at you. I'm not altogether happy about the prospect of what we might find today, either."

And there it was, hanging over them like the blade of a guillotine.

Cara stood and folded her blanket, handing it to him but keeping a careful distance from him as she did. "Guess I better shower so we can get it over with, huh?"

He nodded his agreement, still staring at her, his jaw tight with tension, a small vertical line above the bridge of his nose. He looked very imposing and much too handsome for her own good.

Did fate really have such a cruel sense of humor, she wondered, to have them meet when it was too late, just to torture them both?

It seemed so because this was definitely torture—for her, standing there, remembering the hours of wanting that second kiss he'd had the willpower not to give, of imagining what so much more would be like. And torture for him, standing there like a big, handsome, hard wall of reluctant resolve.

This time it was Cara who took a deep breath and sighed it out. "I don't seem to have much appetite." For food, anyway. "I'll be down in a bit and we can just go."

Then she turned and left him, in spite of everything, taking with her the guilty wish that she'd been awake when he had come downstairs the night before.

THE SECURITY DOOR to the manager's section of the apartment building was propped open when Cara and Quinn arrived, so they went in and knocked on his door.

The man who answered was a small, elderly gentleman with thick, wavy white hair that he obviously took pride in. His gaze went immediately to Cara and he smiled kindly. "Miss Walsh," he greeted. Then amended, "Or should I say Mrs...?"

"Just Cara," she answered.

But before she could say more he glanced at Quinn. "And this must be your new husband?"

"No, this is Quinn Strummel."

By then Quinn had a business card out of his wallet and handed it to the man. As he read it, Quinn said, "I'm afraid Cara has had an accident that's caused her to lose her memory. We've traced her back to the apartment here, but that's about all we know. Anything you could tell us would be of help."

After being reassured she was otherwise all right, the elderly man directed his answers to Quinn. "I'm sorry, there isn't much I can tell you. Cara is a good tenant—quiet, clean. I only found out she was marrying when she gave notice that she'd be moving out."

"And you've never met her fiancé?" Quinn asked.

"No. And she didn't speak of him. Actually, I found it odd that she was marrying when I hadn't seen any one particular male visitor—not that I keep track of everyone's comings and goings, mind you. But usually when one of my tenants is getting married the person they're marrying has been around so much I've begun to recognize them." He turned his attention to Cara. "Do you still plan to move out? I have that apartment leased to a new girl and she expects to move in next week.''

''We'll take care of it,'' Quinn told him, contributing to Cara's peace of mind, as well as the long-winded manager's.

''And there's the bounced check,'' he said, again to Cara.

''The bounced check?'' she repeated.

''I thought that was why you were here. I left a note under your door.''

''We haven't been to the apartment. Cara's purse wasn't recovered so we don't have keys,'' Quinn explained.

''Did a rent check bounce?'' she asked, embarrassed that it might be true and that Quinn should be there to hear it.

''I'm afraid so.''

''Does that happen often?'' Quinn's question seemed purely academic but Cara's insides were still in knots. It hadn't occurred to her that they might find something unpleasant or unsavory about her.

''There was only one other time she couldn't pay the rent, and that was when we made the arrangement.''

''Arrangement?'' Cara hated to keep parroting him but she didn't have the foggiest idea what he was talking about.

''We agreed you could pay half the rent on the first of the month and the other half on the fifteenth in exchange for cleaning the hallway in your section.''

''Was that when she first moved in?''

''Oh, no, she'd been living here for some time by then. In fact, that's why I agreed—she'd been such a good tenant for so many years before that.''

"Do you know what happened to suddenly cause a problem?" Quinn asked.

"She didn't say. But her parents were both killed in a car accident just a few months prior to that. I assumed they must have been helping with her rent, and when they were no longer doing that she came into some financial difficulties. But our arrangement seemed to take care of it. Until now, that is."

"I'm sorry," Cara offered.

"Just make good on it and we'll forget the whole thing," he said with a conspiratorial wink.

Cara squirmed inside. "I hate to ask this, but do you think you could hold off just a little until we can sort through things? At the moment I'm living on the generosity of Mr. Strummel."

The old man looked sideways at Quinn, who didn't seem to be bothered by it.

"Surely there's a damage deposit or something that you could put toward this now?" Quinn urged, his authoritarian demeanor in place once more. It was very effective.

"Yes, there is a damage deposit," the manager finally conceded. "I expected you'd be receiving most of that back. I suppose I could use it for this."

"We'd appreciate it," Quinn said. Then he went on to ask a few more questions, but nothing substantial came of it. Nor was the lease of much help when he persuaded the manager to dig it out of his files. The renter of record was Cara's mother.

"I do know the reason for that," the landlord interjected when he saw the name in the lease. "It seems your folks had a bit of a parting of the ways, though I don't know details or anything like that. Your mother only said that she was so upset over something to do with your father that she felt she had to take time away from him. Lovely woman, your mother. I felt sorry for her. She didn't seem to want to leave your father. Anyway, when they reconciled not long after that, you took the place over and we just never switched the information on the lease.''

Quinn went on to ask if the manager had seen any regular visitors to Cara's and if he could describe them. The landlord couldn't and reiterated that he only came to recognize people who spent a great deal of time visiting, and Cara had had no one like that. He did give them a key to her apartment, though, and told them which car in the lot was hers.

Cara and Quinn thanked him and headed out to the parking lot to have a look at the car before going on to the apartment.

The white station wagon wasn't locked. There wasn't much reason for it to be. It was at least ten years old, and no sane person would have bothered to steal it. The body was rusted out in spots, and it had a bent fender and a broken taillight. And there wasn't anything worth taking on the inside, either, with its split dashboard, threadbare seat covers and relic of a radio.

Quinn sat in the passenger seat, his long legs still on the pavement, and searched the glove box. It held only an owner's manual, a can of instant tire repair and a registration with Cara's name and address on it.

''It's clean,'' she said, trying to find some redeeming quality in the old heap and feeling somewhat discouraged by what she'd learned about herself—her parents were dead, she had financial ills and she drove a car that should be junked.

''Let's check out the apartment,'' Quinn suggested without comment.

It was on the third floor at the back of a green-carpeted hallway that she'd done a good job taking care of, Quinn remarked as he opened the door to her place.

Cara went in first, but not far in. She stopped just clear of the door, where she could see all but the bathroom of the small studio apartment that was dismantled and half-packed.

Looking around, she tried to acquaint herself with the place and summon something in the way of recognition.

The kitchen was to the right of the open space, divided from the rest of the apartment by a breakfast bar with three stools pushed under the white-tile countertop. The living room, which was also the bedroom, held a sofa bed and a wing chair with a big ottoman, all matching one another in a pleasing pale blue plaid upholstery.

There was a beautiful oak coffee table and two identical end tables with white bean-pot lamps on them, a small television and a boom box that seemed to act as a stereo system, an armoire that looked to be an antique and a tiffany lamp hanging over a rolltop desk. And everywhere there were boxes in varying stages of being packed.

"Does it feel like home?" Quinn asked, stepping to her side when he'd closed the door behind them.

"Not really." Though she was happy to find the furniture to her taste and in much better condition than her car. "I hate to say it again, but it's always the same—there's a vague sense of familiarity, but that's all. I'm sorry."

"There's nothing to be sorry for. It's just another one of the pieces we're using to reconstruct your life.

If it clicks for you—great. If not, that's okay, too. We just keep at it.''

"Then I guess we keep at it," she said, grateful for his patience. "Where do we start?"

Quinn surveyed the clutter. "I'll take the kitchen, you check through the bathroom, the places personal things might be. Then we'll go from there until we've been through everything."

"Exploring," she named it, bucking up again.

Quinn headed for the kitchen, and Cara high-stepped her way to the only offshoot of the room—the small bathroom on the other side of two closet doors just beyond the breakfast bar.

It was a nondescript bathroom. There was a box in the sink holding the contents of the medicine cabinet above it. Aspirin, toothpaste, shampoo, a razor, moisturizer, cotton balls and swabs. Ordinary drug-store items that didn't say anything in particular about her.

The vanity below the sink hadn't been emptied yet, but she found only toilet paper, Kleenex and cleaning items, along with a few magazines.

"Big surprise," Quinn called facetiously from the kitchen. "I found chocolate—chocolate cookies, chocolate candy, chocolate milk, even chocolate cof-fee. And some jelly beans—no, not chocolate. They're so sour they make my eyes water," he finished, sound-ing as if he were in pain.

Cara left the bathroom and joined him, popping three of the jelly beans into her mouth and loving them. "Sissy," she taunted.

Most of the cupboards had already been cleaned out, and the boxes on the counters held a pitiful display of pots, pans and groceries.

''You're definitely not a gourmet cook,'' Quinn concluded. Nor was there anything revealing in any of what he'd looked through.

Cara went to the armoire next, while Quinn sat at the desk.

The armoire was exquisite, she decided, running a hand over the flowering vines carved into the front panels. The doors opened at the center and on the inside of each of them was a full-length mirror.

Unlike the wedding gown, the clothes hanging along the pole in the upper section were to Cara's liking. There were some business suits, slacks, silky blouses and two dresses, the latter crushed at one end as if they were rarely worn. All of it was ruffle- and flounce-free, and of good quality, though nothing was new.

A few casual shirts hung there, too, but the majority of her informal clothes—turtleneck T-shirts, sweaters, summer tops, jeans—were folded in the drawers that took up the lower half.

Her shoes were not terribly eclectic, either—a pair of huaraches, some plain flats, suede boots and two pairs of good pumps.

Underwear occupied the lowest drawer, and she was disappointed to discover it all to be functional, conventional and decidedly unsexy—the same as what she'd been wearing beneath her wedding dress, so it shouldn't have surprised her. It did seem strange, though, that even for an occasion like her wedding night she hadn't had great underwear. Was her groom so uninspiring? Because if her groom had been Quinn she would have had on the sheerest, tiniest, laciest . . .

But she couldn't think about that and she forced herself to concentrate on the search.

She went through every drawer, every pocket, every cubbyhole of the armoire so thoroughly she emptied them out and had to put everything back again. But still she found nothing informative.

"How are you doing?" she asked Quinn as she checked the two closets—one containing a vacuum cleaner, broom, dustpan and yardstick, the other a coat closet with two blazers, a winter jacket, an overcoat and a jean jacket in it.

"You're very organized," he answered. "But I'm not coming up with much. Some overdue notices for the utility bills, a bank statement for a checking account—we can follow up on that—pens, pencils, notepad, stationery, paper clips, a pocket calculator, but that's about it."

"Overdue notices?" Cara repeated with yet another grimace as she joined him at the desk.

He handed her the past-due notices and the bank statement, which showed a negative balance. "I'd say we'd be pretty safe in assuming you're in money trouble."

"So much for the heiress theory."

"What I didn't find is an address or phone book, a stub from a paycheck or something that would give us a lead."

"Maybe I don't keep stubs from paychecks and I'm such a whiz at remembering addresses and phone numbers that I don't write them down."

"Possible. But I think it's more likely you carry an address and phone book in your purse." He held up another envelope. "And the animal shelter is sorry not to have received your usual donations, too."

"I can't be all bad if I give to them, can I?"

He glanced up at her. "Who said you were bad?"

"Bounced checks, unpaid bills, a clunker of a car—it isn't a pretty picture."

"It's a picture of someone having some financial problems, nothing else."

"Seems to be some sort of pattern with me, though, if it happened three years ago and again now," she said with a full measure of her disappointment in herself.

"Anything is possible, remember?" he said, not allowing her to be so hard on herself. "Look around this place. You live a conservative life, you aren't reneging on bills to buy yourself fancy clothes at Neiman Marcus or living above your means. There would be shame in that if it were the case. There's no shame in hitting a rough patch—or two."

"That sounds good, but what if I'm a lowlife gambler and what I've hit is a losing streak—again?"

"Don't let your imagination run away with you—*again*," he advised. "There isn't even a lottery ticket around here. You are not a lowlife gambler."

"Oh, sure," she pretended to chastise when she was really grateful for his more understanding perspective. "You're just determined to make me an everyday person instead of something interestingly notorious, aren't you?"

He smiled at that, and she was glad to see his lighter side back within view.

"Last drawer," he said as he pulled it open, showing her what he found as he took each item from it. There were stamps, unused medical-insurance forms, an envelope with the number for a credit card and where to report it lost or stolen, a cash-register receipt for a prescription for nearly two hundred dollars and forty-three dollars in cash in another envelope marked Emergencies.

"Wow, I must have had something really wrong with me to need medicine this expensive," she mused, taking the receipt and finding that while it said Prescription, there were no specifics in the way of a name or number.

"Did you find a prescription bottle anywhere? The label would have your doctor's name on it and that would help."

Cara shook her head. "Nothing. Maybe that was in my purse, too."

"Maybe."

"So how come if I need expensive medicine the doctors at the hospital gave me a clean bill of health?"

"Could be for something that doesn't show up on routine tests, something episodic. Or it could have been a high-priced antibiotic that cured what ailed you." He pushed away from the desk. "At any rate, I need to make two calls while you start going through the boxes. One to cancel your credit card and ask if there's been any activity on it, and the second to the pharmacy to see if they can look up the prescription just from your name."

But Cara was too curious not to follow him to the phone on the kitchen wall and listen while he did those two things.

There hadn't been any recent charges on her credit card, which was good news. The bad news was that she was over her limit and had not as yet paid, despite warnings she'd been sent. Given that, they were only too happy to cancel the card even as Cara grimaced at overhearing yet more discouraging news about herself.

Then Quinn called the pharmacy and gave them her name.

There was no record in their computer system of a prescription of any kind for Cara Walsh.

"That's weird, isn't it?" she asked when he was off the phone.

"It's weird that you'd have the receipt, but beyond that it actually makes more sense if it doesn't belong to you. Otherwise we'd have found the actual label or the bottle itself, or we'd have had some indication that something was wrong with you."

"So if the receipt isn't mine why would I have it?"

"Maybe a friend dropped it and you were just hanging on to it to return."

"Okay," she said dubiously, not having a better explanation.

"At least we don't have to be concerned that you need medicine for something we don't know about. Which means you're as healthy as you look and can get back to work instead of just standing there."

They spent the remainder of the afternoon going through the boxes, finding the stuff of living but nothing that told them anything pertinent. They did come across several framed photographs of people who appeared to be her parents and grandparents, but not one of them was recent or marked with so much as a name or date.

"Seems like I'd have a picture of Peter Whos-its, doesn't it?" she asked as they finished going through the final box without finding one.

"He might be camera shy. It isn't something I'm crazy about."

"And there aren't any photographs of brothers or sisters, either," she noted. "My folks are dead. I imagine my grandparents are. Looks like I'm an orphan."

"Which could help explain why you haven't been reported missing."

"And why I still have my eyebrows and have never licked carpet," she joked. But the humor hid an uneasiness that had grown greater and greater as the search of the apartment obviously drew to a close and she began to wonder if she'd be staying there.

She glanced around, hoping she was wrong and there was something left to go through. "Well, what's next?" she said as if she really thought there might be more.

Quinn took a cursory survey of the place. "Nothing. I don't think we've left any stone unturned."

That's what she was afraid of. "Maybe we should check under all the furniture and the sinks and—"

"What are you thinking now?" he asked, rolling his eyes. "That you have microfilm hidden somewhere because you're really a spy just masquerading as a bride?"

"Well, you never know."

"I have a better idea. Why don't you pack a bag and I'll buy you some dinner on our way home?"

"You mean you aren't going to leave me here?" she asked, relief ringing in her voice.

"Of course not. Until we know who shot you, you aren't safe."

She could have kissed him, though out of gratitude rather than passion this time.

"Besides," he added, sounding somewhat reluctant to admit it, "I'm not ready to lose you."

Okay, maybe she could kiss him with just a little passion.

Instead she grabbed one of the now-empty boxes and went to the armoire to fill it with clothes. "Why don't you let me take *you* to dinner?" she suggested with a nod at the forty-three dollars on the desk.

"That envelope is marked Emergencies. I think you better keep it for that. Dinner is on me."

She considered arguing, but decided against it. The forty-three dollars could be the last money she had to her name. But she swore to herself that she would make all this up to Quinn later on.

While she transferred her things to the packing box, he went to the kitchen. "Let's take your calendar with us and go through it. I noticed when I made the phone calls earlier that you write a lot of things on it." He took it from where it hung on the wall near the telephone. "Aha! Important phone numbers," he said with too much exaggeration for her to take him seriously.

She did glance over at him, though, finding him reading from the back of the large calendar, which sported Georgia O'Keeffe flowers on its upper half.

"Pizza delivery. Italian food. Chinese. And a number for the Original Cookie Company. Do you suppose you've found some place that delivers cookies?"

"No place delivers cookies. Do they?"

"If they do, you've ferreted them out."

She'd packed all she needed by then, including the money, and joined him at the door, where he waited with the calendar. It seemed strange to be so anxious to leave the place that was her home, but she was.

She wasted no time going out into the hallway ahead of Quinn, in her hurry almost bumping into a woman carrying a suitcase in one hand while she jiggled a key in the door to the opposite apartment. Clearly frustrated, she bent to set the suitcase down and caught sight of Cara, startling herself in the process.

"Oh, my God, I didn't know anyone was back there," she said before actually looking at Cara. When she did, she registered more surprise. "Cara? What are you doing here?" she asked, staring for a moment before adding, "I thought you were in Tulsa."

"Do you know me?" Cara asked, then thought what a silly question that was when they were obviously neighbors.

The woman looked at her as if she'd gone mad. "Do I know you?" she repeated.

She was a tall, large-boned woman, no less elegant for her size, with beautiful, close-cropped blond hair and crystal-clear blue eyes that rose to Quinn as he stepped to Cara's side, introduced himself and held out one of his cards.

She took it, but didn't look at it, concentrating instead on Quinn's brief explanation of Cara's amnesia.

"You have to be kidding," the woman said, not unkindly but with a doubting laugh as she turned back to her harried jiggling of the key. "Amnesia? Like in a soap opera or something? Is that a joke?" she said, finally managing to open the door.

"No, it's not a joke," Quinn answered, his voice an octave louder to reach her as she hurried inside, flinging her suitcase on a nearby chair.

Her apartment was identical to Cara's, and she dashed into the kitchen and snatched something from a drawer that she stashed in the pocket of the jacket she wore before rushing back to the living room.

"We'd appreciate talking to you," he said, even though they'd clearly lost her full attention to disbelief. "Could you start by telling us your name?"

"I'm Nancy Sommers," she called as she took an artist's portfolio from where it was propped against the end of the breakfast bar. "Look, I don't know what kind of game this is, but I can't play along. I'm already late for an interview for the job of a lifetime. Damn plane was delayed three hours, if you can imagine," she finished as she came back out.

"We aren't joking and this isn't a game," Quinn repeated more forcefully. "And it's very important that we get any information we can on Cara."

"Nothing is as important as this interview. Sorry, but that's how it is," she said, punctuating her finality by firmly closing the door behind her.

"Afterward, then," Quinn persisted.

"You mean like tonight? No," she said with a grimace. "I've been out of town since Friday. I'll call you tomorrow and you can explain just what you're talking about," she said with a wave of Quinn's card as she jogged away from them, nearly flew down the stairs and went out the security entrance.

"I think she's in a hurry," Cara understated.

"Your memory may be a dud but your powers of observation are in good form."

"Do you think I'm supposed to be honeymooning in Tulsa?" she asked as they followed Nancy Sommers' path out of the building.

"Not the honeymoon capital of the world," he agreed. "But if she knows you well enough to know that, she probably knows a lot more we can use. We'll talk to her tomorrow. In the meantime we have a calendar to go through and some dinner to eat. How does pizza sound?"

THE RESTAURANT he took her to was really just a bar with a few booths around the edges. It looked pretty seedy, but Cara didn't want to mention it.

Her silence was rewarded by incredible pizza with a crust that tasted like beer and butter. She and Quinn both sat on one side of the bench seat so they could share the search through the calendar while they ate their pizza.

She didn't lead a busy social life, that was apparent right off the bat. There were a few birthdays and occasional lunches or dinners with people whose first names alone were noted. Appointments were even less frequent, and those merely said Doctor or Dentist or Haircut rather than giving any more information.

The only name that appeared with frequency was Tillie.

Tillie's Birthday, Tillie's Anniversary and numerous dates on which just Tillie was written.

Tillie, they assumed, was a good friend.

As with the photographs at the apartment, what was glaringly absent from the calendar was anything marked Peter, including a birthday. Stranger still, on the preceding Saturday there was a single word: Wedding. And there wasn't anything at all in the way of preparation before it. Not a bridal shower, or a meeting with a caterer or so much as a reminder to send out invitations.

"Maybe I was just a proxy bride," Cara suggested on the way home. "Maybe the real bride is an overseas correspondent or an undercover operative for the CIA or—"

"A proxy bride?" he repeated with a laugh, cutting her off before she got too far into another of her flights of fancy. "Not likely. But it is strange that Peter Whos-its didn't get a single mention anywhere and that a wedding that commanded a two-thousand-dollar dress didn't have something leading up to it."

"I don't like what I'm thinking," she admitted.

"Let's hear it."

"I was just adding up what we've found today. No pay stub could mean I'm unemployed, which would also account for the bounced check and not being able to meet my bills. I don't have any family to turn to for help. What I do have is a fiancé who can afford a two-thousand-dollar wedding dress." Cara paused as they pulled into the garage and Quinn stopped the engine. "What if I'm a gold digger? What if I was marrying for money rather than love? What if that's why I don't seem to have any emotional ties to keep me from being attracted to—"

This time she cut herself off, embarrassed by what she'd almost said. "Maybe I'm just a cold, calculating opportunist," she reiterated to cover her tracks, getting out of the car as she did.

Quinn followed suit, taking her box of clothes from the trunk before trailing her to the house. "I don't believe you're a gold digger and I know for a fact that you aren't cold or calculating," he said as he opened the back door and waited for her to go in.

"How about just plain desperate?" she asked, grateful that he hadn't commented on her slip of the tongue.

He apparently considered desperation a possibility because he didn't deny it. He didn't say anything as he set the box on the kitchen table.

Cara took a deep breath that puffed her cheeks to balloons and blew it out elaborately. "I'm tired of wondering about it all today. It's making my head spin," she said, going into the living room, where she kicked off her shoes, lay down on the floor and propped her feet on the coffee table.

When she glanced up she found Quinn standing above her, grinning at her. "What are you doing?"

Good question, she thought as she realized she had just naturally gotten into a position that had her body at the same angle it would have been in if she were sitting in a chair, except her back was pressed flat to the carpet. "I don't know," she admitted, "but it sure feels good after so many hours hunched over boxes. Try it."

He gave a little laugh and then, as if on a whim, joined her.

The only free space that allowed that kind of access to the coffee table was right where Cara was, so he had to lie beside her.

So close beside her that his leg brushed hers. But she tried not to notice. Or like the feel of it as much as she did.

"What we need are stars to look up at," he said.

"Close your eyes and imagine them," she suggested.

She took her own advice but it wasn't stars she saw when she did. It was Quinn as he'd been a moment before, standing over her. And as if she were looking at the real thing instead of just a mental image, she could vividly see up the long length of his muscular legs spread apart just slightly, to narrow hips and waist, to the broadening V of his chest where his arms had been crossed, to those mile-wide shoulders that she longed to trace with her palms, to his strong neck and sharp jaw, his supple mouth that felt even better than it looked, his sleek nose and those silver eyes....

So vivid was the picture in her mind that she thought she could actually feel his heated gaze on her.

Then she realized that her sense of that was too strong to be coming only from her imagination and she peeked to find him studying her, a small frown on his handsome face.

"You're not stargazing," she said.

"No, I'm not."

"What are you doing?"

"The same thing I did last night when you were asleep—watching you and wondering how anybody can make me feel as good and as mixed up as you do. All at the same time."

And it clearly troubled him. "Should I apologize?" she asked in a quiet tone that was more serious than she'd intended.

But it wasn't her question he answered. "Things are crazy inside of me. I want you and I don't want to want you. I know I shouldn't want you. But every time I look at you or hear the sound of your voice, or even just think about you, it's like stepping from a cold, dark room into summer sunshine, and no matter what should be or what I've vowed or how much I fight it, I need to reach out to it, soak it up, make it mine...make *you* mine."

"That doesn't sound like anything I'm sorry for," she confessed in a barely audible voice.

His eyes held hers for a long moment. Then he brought one of those giant hands to her hair and down to her nape as he rolled to his side and did what she'd wanted so much for him to do the night before—he kissed her.

Should or shouldn't, it didn't matter as she raised a palm to the side of his neck, finding steel encased in sleek, masculine skin.

His mouth opened over hers and she matched it, eager for that tongue that only traced the bare interior of her lips, teasing and slowly learning, savoring, lingering until she met it with her own and invited him inside.

Lord, but the man could kiss!

And Cara couldn't help wondering how much more he might be good at.

Her back floated off the floor just enough for him to slip his arms all the way around her, to wrap her in an embrace that tore down the barriers between them.

Cara slipped her own arms around him, around the wide span of those shoulders to the hard mounds and valleys of his back where the muscles shifted with every hungry movement of his mouth over hers.

She could go on kissing him forever, she thought, and even if she could never know more of him than that, it was glorious enough to make it almost all right.

Their breath mingled, their tongues played and courted and then grew serious, seductive, suggestive, slowly thrusting in and out, raising mental images more powerful even than she'd had before. Delicious, erotic images that arched her back even more and tightened her arms around him, pressing her breasts against him, straining, yearning, achingly alive and aroused and craving his touch, craving to be free of the clothes that kept her bare flesh from his....

But just then, just when she was nearly writhing beneath him, he stopped.

Cara looked up at him, hardly able to believe it.

His jaw was as taut as a rip cord as he tipped his forehead to hers.

"So much for hands off," he said in a ragged, raspy voice.

Cara fought for control, a battle as fierce as trying to stem high tide, as waves of desire washed through her, consumed her, made her think that nothing could possibly be as important as being in this man's arms.

But a more rational part of her reminded her that she didn't have the right to be there. Not when only a few days before she'd been dressed in a wedding gown bought by another man.

Quinn let go of her and stood, offering her a hand to help her up, but taking it away again the moment she was on her feet, as if just that much contact could shatter his willpower.

He jammed his fingers through his hair and in the same stern, tormented tone that had been in his voice that morning, said, "I'm going for a walk. Do us both a favor and don't be down here when I get back. Be in your room with the door locked."

He didn't wait for her to agree or disagree. He just went out the front of the house on determined strides.

Fleetingly Cara considered ignoring his order. She considered spending the time he was gone to light candles, to strip down to nothing but one of his big shirts left unbuttoned to her navel, to lie in wait for him to come back.

But she didn't do any of that.

She went upstairs and slipped into her own lonely bed, where she listened for his return.

It didn't come for nearly an hour. And when it did she heard him bypass his bedroom to stand outside hers.

That wicked part of her urged him to come in to her as every inch of her cried out for him.

But he didn't even try the door.

Instead, after a moment he backtracked to his own room.

And even though she knew he was right to do it, disappointment and unsatisfied desire were cold companions.

Chapter Six

Cara made sure she was up before Quinn the next morning so she could have breakfast waiting for him for a change. She wasn't much of a whiz in the kitchen but by the time he got downstairs she had a passable meal ready.

French toast, a good old American fruit salad, eggs scrambled with Canadian bacon she'd found in the fridge and Colombian coffee—an international breakfast, she announced as she guided Quinn to the table like a maître d', even holding his chair out for him.

"You're a nut, do you know it?" he said but with amusement in his voice in spite of the solemn expression he'd had on his face when he'd first come in—no doubt the result of the restless night he'd spent pacing his room. Cara knew because she'd been unable to sleep herself and had lain in bed listening. And hoping...

But she didn't want to think about that.

"So what detecting are we doing today?" she asked when she sat across the table from him.

He tasted her cooking first, pronounced it good and then said, "There are two things on today's agenda— we go to the bank with your checking-account statement and ask to see your canceled checks. I don't know how your bank works, but mine keeps them all on microfilm rather than storing the actual checks. If that's the case we'll have to go through them there.''

"What do you expect to find?"

He shrugged one of those broad shoulders encased in a crisp white shirt that set off the dark mink color of his hair. "We might come up with a doctor's name or the full name of a friend, or, who knows, just something we'll be able to follow up on."

"And the second thing on today's agenda?"

"We're going to track down your marriage license. We should be able to do that with your name alone, and it will give us Peter Whos-its's last name so we can stop calling him Peter Whos-its."

Except that it wasn't only a matter of what to call him, and Cara knew it. No doubt the marriage license would also give his address, which, in turn, could make him one phone call or one drive away.

She didn't want to think about that either.

Instead, she rolled her eyes and groaned. "More legwork? Where are the chills, thrills and excitement of P.I. work?"

He laughed. "Sorry, hotshot, I know how you must be itching for some action, but legwork is the basis of the job. Chills, thrills and excitement are in short supply."

THE BOOKKEEPING department of the bank was in a dreary subbasement. Quinn had been right about the checks being on microfilm, so they settled in to go through the last four years' worth, taking two years apiece. Quinn said he was hoping to find out if there was a connection between her financial ills of three years ago and the current ones.

They each made a list of checks written that weren't for rent, utilities or regular payments, noting her doctor's name, her dentist's, anything or anyone whom they might be able to contact for information about her.

They also noted patterns, which was how they discovered that beginning three years earlier Cara began writing checks every month to something called Springfield, as well as the fact that at the same time she started paying two phone bills and two gas-and-electric bills each month. And within the past year, there were also regular checks written to the pharmacy, though there were no records of prescriptions for her.

"I lead a double life?" Cara postulated with mock drama as they left the bank late that afternoon to make a hurried drive to the city and county buildings. "What if I'm one of those people with multiple personalities? What if it isn't really amnesia I have, but just a blackout of the other personalities that have been living my life until now? What if I'm just a new personality that's emerged?"

One glance at Quinn in the driver's seat told her he was fighting a huge grin. "If your multiple personalities can all live in one body, why couldn't they all live in one apartment?"

"Maybe one of them has something going on at another place."

"Using the same name and checking account? The only thing I know about multiple personalities is what I've seen on talk shows, but I'm reasonably sure in cases like that each personality has their own name.

Besides, we haven't found anything that points to you being more than one person.''

Okay, so it did seem like a stretch, but she'd only been fractionally serious, anyway. "What's your theory then?'' she challenged.

"You're supporting someone,'' he answered simply enough. "Springfield must be an apartment house or maybe some sort of institution, though the phone and utility bills make me lean more toward an apartment.''

Cara's imagination went from the fantastic to the tragic. "Maybe I have a beautiful but ill sister who secludes herself somewhere, living a hermit's life.''

Quinn surprised her by agreeing with that one. "You might not be completely off base. It certainly looks like you've taken over supporting someone who isn't altogether well because you're paying out a lot of money for medicine that isn't yours.''

That took Cara from her wandering imaginings back down to earth as something else occurred to her. "Then somebody really could be depending on me,'' she said, all joking aside.

Quinn's only answer was the acknowledgment of raised eyebrows when he glanced over at her again.

"What if they're in jeopardy because I'm not around?''

"They aren't.''

"How can you be so sure?''

"Because you're supposed to be in Tulsa on a honeymoon. I'm sure if any of this is even the case, that you provided for whoever you left behind while you were gone. Plus the utility bills suggest a private residence of some kind, which means whoever it is must be at least partially self-sufficient. And remember, no one has missed you or they'd have reported it.'' He paused and then repeated, "That's if—and that's a big if—any of this is even the case. Right now it's just supposition. So relax."

She had tensed up, she realized. And he was right. While there might be a few signs pointing to the scenario of someone being dependent on her, it was still only marginally more likely than anything else. "Well, if any of it is true," she said then, more brightly, "at least it means I'd have a good reason to be a gold digger."

"Which we also don't know you are," he reminded as he found a parking spot and they headed into the maze of government buildings.

The marriage license was filed and listed information they already knew about Cara. Peter was Peter Shelby, and his address was a very upscale area in Cherry Creek—an all-around upscale offshoot of Denver where property values were sky-high.

What wasn't registered was a marriage certificate, though the clerk cautioned them that that didn't necessarily mean the wedding hadn't taken place. It was possible the document just hadn't reached them yet or been recorded.

Cara and Quinn thanked the youthful man, who had stayed past closing time to help them.

It was late by then and several courtrooms, as well as the offices, were spilling people from all directions. In the crush neither Quinn nor Cara said much as they made their way outside.

There was already a traffic jam in the parking lot, and they weaved between cars to find Quinn's, which was nose first against a low brick wall that separated the lot from the street.

Cara stood nearby as Quinn unlocked the passenger door. He'd just opened it for her when they both heard her name called from across the street. They looked up to find a man in a well-tailored suit waving to get her attention. He had one foot inside a red sedan as if he'd spotted her just as he was catching a ride with his car pool. And he didn't look even remotely familiar to her.

"Hey," he shouted over four lanes of traffic and the horn that honked because he was taking too long to get in. "I was happy to hear you ditched that dumb wedding and old Put-down Peter! I'll call you for lunch soon."

"Wait!" Quinn hollered, leaping over the wall and running out into traffic to catch him. But the other man apparently didn't hear him, slipping into the car just before it pulled around the corner and disappearing without anyone inside seeming to realize Quinn was trying to reach them.

Fate was having a heyday with them, Cara thought as she and Quinn got in his car and he backed out of the spot.

"Did you recognize him?" he asked.

"Not at all," she answered.

Getting through the parking lot was more stopping and waiting than actually moving, and as they made their slow progress Cara considered what the man across the street had said. "Put-down Peter?" she repeated. "My groom is sounding better and better."

"Don't take too seriously what a rival thinks."

"Who says that man was a rival?"

"He's glad you didn't get married and he can't wait to take you to lunch—sounds like a rival to me."

And was that just a hint of jealousy in his tone? Cara was delighted. But she didn't say anything about it.

"What do you suppose it means that I *ditched* the wedding?" she asked instead.

"Probably just that you didn't show up—due to a bullet wound to the head and an unplanned trip to the mountains."

When Quinn finally maneuvered out of the lot he headed in the same direction the other car had gone and even went up and down all the cross streets. There was no sign of the red sedan, and since the street led directly to the highway it was a pretty good bet the man who'd called Cara's name was long gone.

"So what now?" she asked as they took that same highway home.

"We hit the phone book again—see what Springfield is." Then he added a little belatedly, "And if there's a number for Peter Shelby."

"And then what?" she asked with the same reluctance.

He waited a moment before answering. "One of us could call him, see what kind of a response we get, arrange a meeting."

She was glad he hadn't suggested just showing up on the guy's doorstep. But it was only a small relief. The fact was, they were closing in on her life.

Neither of them said much more the rest of the way to Quinn's house. When they got there he took out the phone books and without much trouble found a number for a place called Springfield. Springfield was a retirement community.

"I just assumed my grandparents were no longer living. Maybe I was wrong."

"Just about anything is possible. Whoever is at Springfield could be an aunt or uncle or a mentor or just an elderly friend, too."

But there was something that told Cara that the person at Springfield was one of her grandparents. And something else that made her feel an inviting warmth at the thought of going there and finding out.

But then she realized that this sense was the same as she'd had over the house off the highway, which had proved to mean nothing, so she cautioned herself not to take it too seriously.

"Springfield is in Arvada, not far from your apartment. We could go out there tonight but I think we'd be better off waiting until tomorrow. If whoever runs the place doesn't know you by sight, we'll need to knock on some doors and daytime is more conducive to that."

Which neatly tucked away one of today's discoveries. But that still left Peter Shelby.

Neither Quinn nor Cara said it. They didn't have to.

Quinn took a deep breath and opened the residential phone book to the *S*'s.

"He's listed," he said a moment later.

"Put-down Peter?" Cara said before she even knew she was going to, her tone rife with reluctance again.

"What do you want to do?" Quinn asked after silence ticked away some time.

She wanted to pretend they'd never found out anything about him. Not his last name. Not his address. Not any of the unpleasant aspects of his personality. She wanted to go into the living room the way she had when they'd come in the night before, lie down on the floor and reenact what they'd done then, though without stopping short of anything.

But she knew she was just procrastinating.

She shrugged as if this weren't the hardest thing she'd done since awakening in that mountain meadow. "I guess I'll call him."

She could feel Quinn drawing into himself, giving her space to do what she had to do. But it didn't make it any easier.

This time it was Cara who took a deep breath as she went to the phone on the wall. "Read me the number."

Quinn did.

As she stood there listening to the rings, Cara realized every muscle in her body was tensed. And though she would have liked to believe it was from the fear that Peter Shelby was who had shot her, she knew the reason was that no matter what had been between them before, now that she knew Quinn it could never be the same.

A click on the other end of the line cut off the rings, but it wasn't a person who answered. It was an insufferable male voice on a machine.

"You've reached the residence of Peter and Sheila Shelby. Mother and I are currently in Tulsa but if you'll leave a message at the sound of the tone, your call will be attended to by our staff and appropriately relayed to us when we return on Thursday. Thank you."

Cara wasn't sure whether or not to say anything but finally blurted out, "This is Cara. Please call me." She gave Quinn's phone number, then hung up, digesting the answering-machine message that had sounded ridiculously stuffy.

"Well?" Quinn prompted.

"He lives with his mother and he took her on my honeymoon." And with that said, Cara couldn't help laughing at the absurdity of it.

She pressed the redial button on the phone, stretched the cord to Quinn and handed him the receiver. "Here, listen."

He did. Then he handed it back to her to hang up, smiling a little himself. "It does sound that way."

"He also doesn't seem too broken up about my 'ditching' the wedding." Then she remembered that Quinn considered Peter Shelby a suspect. "Unless maybe you're right about him being the one who shot me. Maybe he really wanted to take his mother on the honeymoon instead, so he plugged me and dumped me in the mountains."

"*Plugged* you? What did you do the other night, stay up and watch old detective movies?"

"Just one."

"Besides," he said, laughing now, "you weren't plugged. You were grazed."

"But still, he couldn't have been too heartbroken, to take his mother on the honeymoon."

"He sounds like a lot of things, but heartbroken isn't one of them, no," Quinn agreed.

Cara felt remarkably better to know it. She also felt a great deal of relief that she was not going to have to deal with Peter Shelby immediately. "Should I have said something more than I did? Like where I am or that I have amnesia?" she wondered aloud.

Quinn shook his head. "You did just fine. It's better if we talk to him directly when he gets back."

And that was that for the moment.

Quinn wrote down the address for Springfield and put away the phone books, while Cara watched him and thought about the long night stretching out in front of them.

"So," she said with a sigh when he'd finished. "Now that we've done all we can for today, what do we do with the evening?" Somehow that sounded more suggestive than she'd intended.

Quinn seemed to glance around, and she had the sense he wasn't too sure they could be trusted spending the time alone in the house.

Or was it just that *she* wasn't too sure they could be trusted spending the time alone in the house?

"How do you feel about a night picnic?" he asked.

"I don't know if I've ever been on one before, but it's an interesting idea."

"There's a park not far from here. It has a big lake with a path around it, a lot of picnic tables, tennis courts...."

In other words, they'd be out in public. "Great. We can make sandwiches, walk around the lake...." *Behave ourselves.*

"Sounds like a good idea."

"Then let's do it."

Working together, they were on their way within a half hour, just as the sun began to set in glorious colors. Brilliant oranges, golds and umbers, it was like an autumn explosion in the sky over the mountains as the last yellow rays of sunshine speared their way up to silhouette the tall peaks.

Cara and Quinn set their picnic gear in a spot slightly back from the lake amidst a horseshoe of tall, thick-boled oak trees. Then they headed for the path, walking facing nature's spectacular display so they wouldn't miss that last burst of color before darkness crept in and took over.

"I wonder if I've lived in Colorado all my life and always enjoyed this as much as I do now?" Cara mused out loud. But she could feel Quinn's gaze on her rather than on the sunset. "You're missing it," she said, glancing up at him.

"Not really," he told her with a smile. "Watching you enjoy it so much is something to see, too. Your eyes are lit up like a kid's at Christmas."

"Am I being silly?"

"Not at all. Actually I was thinking how nice it is."

There were some things she thought were pretty nice, too. Him, for one. And walking beside him as he kept a pace slow enough not to outdistance her on legs so much longer. And the sound of his deep, resonant voice for her ears alone. And the warm thrill of just having him near.

That was almost too nice.

She studied the sunset again. "You know what else I'm really enjoying?"

"What?"

"Playing detective."

"No. I never would have guessed," he said facetiously but not unkindly. "And here I thought all those wild imaginings of yours were coming out of hating the job."

"Maybe," she postulated once more, "no matter what I've done before, I'll quit and become a P.I. myself. Want another partner?" she teased, once again glancing at him, though this time a bit coyly, from the corner of her eye.

"You're too much of a distraction," he flirted back just a little dryly.

"In a good way or a bad one?"

"A good one."

"Thank you." That was genuine, but then she teased again, "Maybe if you won't have me I'll open up my own agency and give you a run for your money."

"I might have you, just not as a partner P.I.," he countered, dishing out a little of his own.

She smiled over at him. "But you're not worried that I'd be stiff competition?"

"Might be fun," he said in a way that didn't sound as if business was on his mind at all.

They'd rounded the lake by then, the sky had turned to cobalt and most of the other people in the park were heading out. Cara and Quinn spread the blanket they'd brought and sat down to dinner and a bottle of wine.

"So tell me how you became a P.I.," she urged after they'd begun to eat.

"It was the natural progression from being a cop."

"But why progress at all when you were a good cop? I saw the decorations on your bookcase that first night you brought me home."

"Being a good cop ran in the family. My father was a good cop. Logan is a good cop, even though he's having a bad time right now. That doesn't mean it was good for *me*."

"Did your father push you into it, like a family business?"

"He didn't push, no. But he liked the work and was proud of it. We were all proud of him. I guess I just wanted to be a part of that."

"So how come you quit?"

"Frustration," he said simply, but the word alone rang with a wealth of that feeling.

It was dark by then and Cara had eaten her fill. She put the remnants of her food back in the small cooler they'd carried in with them, keeping only her wine.

"What frustrated you?" she persisted.

"You would have, for instance."

That confused her. "Me?"

"If I'd been a cop when I'd found you, I would have had to take you to the hospital, file a report that turned you over to missing persons, who would have, in turn, called social services and that would have been the last of it. What happened from there would have been completely out of my hands." He paused and his expression turned very serious. "And sometimes when that happened, things didn't work out very well," he finished.

His strong brow was beetled so severely it looked dangerous. Not that Cara was afraid of him, but some people probably should be, she thought.

Then, as if he'd lost his appetite, he discarded half of his meal, too. Like Cara, he hung on to only the paper cup that held his wine. He stretched his legs out, crossed them at the ankles and leaned back on his free hand.

He'd changed into a red polo shirt and a pair of tennis shorts before they left, and in order to straighten his legs he had to position them at a diagonal just off Cara's right knee where she sat Indian fashion. Even in the shadows cast by the trees she could see the dark hair that speckled each muscular thigh and grew denser down his perfect calves. It made her mouth go a little dry.

She drank more wine and forced her thoughts back to what he'd said.

"Was there something in particular that made you decide to stop being a cop?"

He didn't answer right away, but when he did, he downplayed it. "There was a kid. A runaway."

"A girl?"

He chuckled mirthlessly. "She reminded me of Lindsey." He looked pointedly at Cara, the shadows of his eyes penetrating her. "People reminding me of my sister seem to get me into a lot of trouble," he added with wry amusement.

"Me?"

He didn't confirm or deny that. "Anyway," he went on, "I kept having to haul this kid in. Smart mouthed, contrary, ornery, quick as a whip, bright, beautiful, tough as nails—or so she wanted everybody to think. And a hell of a good pickpocket," he said with grudging admiration.

"But not a good enough pickpocket not to get caught."

"Actually, I'd catch her when she sold the stuff— rings, watches, credit cards. She had pride, you see— she wouldn't resort to prostitution the way a lot of runaways do just to eat or get in out of the cold. In her own way, I guess she'd developed a skill to keep her life a little more palatable."

"So what happened to her?"

Again there was that heavy pause. "I'd haul her in, book her and that was the end of my part. I was a cop, I had a job to do and it didn't include anything after that. I tried to talk to social services, to convince them to give her some special attention, find her a foster home that would really put some effort into channeling her energies in the right direction, a place that would roll with some of her attitude and stick with her long enough to get to what was underneath it. But that never happened, and the next thing I'd know, she was on the streets and I was arresting her again."

His hesitation this time was punctuated with a slow, sad shake of his head. "She finally picked the wrong pocket. She died in an alley downtown."

"I'm sorry," Cara said quietly.

"Me, too."

"What would you do with that same kid now? As a P.I.?"

He shrugged. "I don't know. Except that I wouldn't let her fall through the cracks in the system."

"Maybe you'd take her in yourself," Cara mused, thinking of her own situation. She found it difficult to consider what had happened to her in a bad light since she'd been fortunate enough to have been rescued by him. She knew, too, that no matter what had brought that girl to the life of a runaway, she'd have been better off if Quinn had been free to help her the way he would have liked to.

For a few moments they both stared at the lake, where moonbeams rippled on the water's glassy top. No more sounds drifted into their woodsy enclave—no dogs barking as their owners walked them, no kids' laughter, no adult voices goading volleyball opponents. Cara doubted that she and Quinn were actually all alone, but it seemed that way. And the deep shadows cast over them by the trees only increased that sense.

"So you became a P.I.," she said, rather than thinking all the things that the feeling of seclusion was making her think.

"Mostly, I became not a cop," Quinn amended. "I became somebody who didn't have to follow rules that kept me from finishing things the way I thought they should be finished. Nobody tells me when to stop now.

Or how much I can or can't do. Or where I have to draw the line. I make those decisions."

"Including taking amnesiacs into your own home, where they cause you trouble," she added in a lighter note.

He tossed what remained of his wine into the grass and put the cup in the cooler with the rest of their dinner things. Then, braced on one elbow, facing her, he said, "I didn't say you caused me trouble. I said you got me into trouble. Internal trouble. And a whole new kind of frustration."

"I'm sor—"

He stopped her with his fingertips to her lips. "Don't say it," he ordered. "Don't apologize because you make me feel the way you do."

His finger against her mouth seemed like a caress and set off sparks deep inside of her that flared into flames when he slid his hand to the side of her neck.

"Now I'm even breaking my own rules," he said in a quiet rumble of a voice.

"Which ones?" she asked in a barely audible voice as she tried to gain some control over her racing heart.

"Rule number one: Don't get involved with the client."

He was doing a slow massage of her neck that inched his hand up into her hair, and she had to swallow to get her voice through all he was awakening in her with just that simple touch. "Seems to me you stopped being a cop so you could get more involved with people."

"Not personally involved."

"Are you personally involved?"

"Heart and soul," he admitted reluctantly.

"Mind and body?" Had she died out in that meadow, she thought, she probably would have danced with the devil, for something in her seemed to keep urging her to tempt fate. At least where Quinn was concerned.

"Heart and soul and mind..."

She wanted his body, too. The whole long, lean, muscular length of it.

Maybe they'd overestimated how safe it was to be out in the open air of the park.

His hand slid away from her neck to take her wineglass. He drained what remained in it and set it in the cooler. Then his hand came back, this time diving purposefully into her hair to her nape to pull her toward him as he raised up and met her halfway.

But he didn't kiss her immediately. For a moment his eyes bored into hers, so close that Cara could see their silver shine even in the density of the shadows that secluded them. She could feel the heat of his breath, and then he captured her mouth with his, even as he eased her back, to lie partially beneath that big body he'd yet to commit to her.

Cara needed no coaxing to wrap her arms around the wide span of his shoulders, to press her palms against his steely back as she wondered what it would look like without a shirt, knowing it must be magnificent to see because it was magnificent to feel.

His mouth over hers was wide open, hungry, insistent, as his tongue plunged home, starting up where he'd left off the night before as if they'd never stopped.

The urgency between them was instant. Their mouths worked madly and both Cara's hands rose to his head, into his hair, holding him to the kiss that was driving her wild.

One of his massive thighs crossed her lap, bringing her close to the hard ridge at her hip that told her exactly how much he wanted her, and the first press of it against her made her groan with needs of her own.

She was straining against him, straining for him, for more of him, hating the clothes that kept them apart, not caring if they were in only the relative privacy of the trees and shadows.

But despite those clothes, they were moving together in a slow, rhythmic, erotic dance as he cupped her derriere and held her tightly to him. Then that hand slid up and pulled her shirt free of her jeans to find its way inside to splay across her bare back.

Oh, but it was so good to feel even that much of his skin on hers!

But it got better as he traced a path around to her breast, left braless in the shirt that was so loose she hadn't thought she needed one today. Now she counted that fact as a blessing as his palm covered her naked nipple and taught it to kernel into a tight knot of desire. If she'd ever felt anything so wonderful, she didn't remember it and her back arched into the magic he was working.

His mouth abandoned hers to kiss her chin, to slide to the soft, sensitive underside, to trail a path down the column of her neck. He nudged his way into the open top buttons of her blouse, nibbling her collarbone, tracing the lowest hollow of her throat with his tongue.

Cara let her head fall back, thrusting her breast even farther into his hand in invitation to what her body was crying out for—his mouth over her engorged nipple.

But he never made it.

Instead he rolled his head back, away from her, inhaling a barrel-deep breath of agony as he did.

"I want to take you home, take you to bed and make love to you all night long," he told her in a ragged voice.

But something about the way he said it let her know it wasn't going to happen. No matter how much she wanted it to.

Then he confirmed it when he took his hand out of her shirt, pulling it down with yet another sigh that sounded slightly more in control.

"But I won't," he finished, taking his leg away, too, and with it, his lower half.

Cara was still catching her own breath and fighting the needs raging inside of her. All she could manage to say was "Oh."

It made him laugh just a little. Or maybe he was laughing at himself or the two of them or life in general. But he pulled her head to his chest as if he couldn't resist holding her and yet couldn't trust their bodies next to each other.

"I can't make love to you until we know the whole story, Cara. Until we know you won't regret it."

"I wouldn't regret it," she heard herself say.

"You would if you got your memory back and realized you're in love with old Peter Whos-its. You'd regret it a lot. You'd go back feeling rotten. And I can't let that happen. Not to you. Not to me."

She could feel the pounding of his heart beneath her brow, and every inch of her cried out for him. But she knew he was right, that an act between them that would be wonderful right now could be sullied by what they discovered later on. And she didn't want that, either.

She pulled away from him and sat up, staring out at the lake. "I don't believe I'm in love with him," she said quietly, but with conviction.

"But we can't be sure of that. And until we are—"

"I agree with you. I just wanted you to know."

He nodded.

For a while they both watched the play of moonlight on the water, and Cara willed her raging senses back into submission with no small amount of effort.

Then Quinn stood and offered her a hand up.

She took it, but once she was on her feet he let go. They were both careful to keep some distance between them as they gathered their picnic gear and went home in a silence that kept them safely apart.

"I have some paperwork to do in my office," Quinn claimed when they were inside again, but Cara knew it was more an attempt to keep them on the straight and narrow than a call to duty. "Why don't you get some rest?" he suggested.

"I think I will," she said, as if it was a good idea.

They went as far as his office door together, and there she glanced at him to say a benign good-night. But it wasn't easy to disengage her gaze from his as he responded in kind. Until he pointed in the direction of the stairs with a commanding rise of his chin.

"See you tomorrow," she said, finally going on without him.

But when she reached the upper level she couldn't help pausing a moment at his room, just far enough inside to smell the scent of his after-shave that lingered in the air, to see his big quilt-covered bed, to wonder what it would be like to be there with him at that moment....

It was an exercise in self-torture as every desire reawakened instantly.

Swallowing it all, she forced herself back out into the hallway, on to her own room, where she closed the door. And there, in that unwitnessed moment, she laid her cheek against the wood, imagining it was Quinn's chest.

God, how she wanted him!

She didn't know how she was going to get through another frustration-filled night.

The only way she could do it, she thought, was to hope that what the next day brought would set her free.

Chapter Seven

As Cara stood in front of the bathroom mirror the following morning to French-braid her hair, she thought that she was almost getting used to the odd sense that washed through her each time she looked at her own reflection.

It wasn't that her face was still unfamiliar to her— she'd come to know it well again. But there was definitely something about seeing herself that yanked hard on the stubborn door that closed away her memory.

She couldn't help wondering if that door was ever going to open. And if it did, what would come flooding through it.

Were feelings a part of memory?

That was what preyed on her mind most.

Was it possible that she was deeply in love with the man named Peter Shelby, and the moment her memory returned, so would that love?

It just didn't seem possible.

But as Quinn so often told her, anything was possible.

And if it should happen, where would that put her feelings for Quinn?

She was venturing into dangerous territory to think about that, she silently told her reflection as she applied a little mascara to her lashes. Everything was so precarious, she'd actually been trying to avoid considering that she even had feelings for him. But after a night spent almost sleepless with wanting him, she knew that not to think about the feelings didn't make them nonexistent. It didn't even lessen their power.

And they were very powerful.

She cared for him. So much that it made true what she'd told him the night before—she didn't believe she loved her fiancé.

How could she? Maybe anything was possible, but of all the things she'd learned about herself, about her life, all she'd postulated, the most difficult to accept was that she could be feeling all she was for Quinn if she honestly loved another man.

Because if she loved anyone, it was Quinn.

Now she really was on dangerous ground.

But how could she help loving him? And not because he'd rescued her. No, this didn't have anything to do with her baby-duck-bonding theory of early on. What she felt for him now wasn't connected to dependency. It was the man himself who inspired what was happening. The man she'd come to know as honorable and honest and ethical and kind and compassionate and strong and fun to be with and...okay, and great looking and so sexy that one glance at him raised her blood pressure.

Was it possible, she wondered then, that Quinn was so dynamic in his appeal that he'd just overshadowed even genuine affection for her fiancé?

All right, all right, anything was possible.

But she doubted it.

For how could what she was feeling for Quinn have grown in a heart already full?

She just couldn't imagine it.

But then, she couldn't imagine that she wrote bad checks or left bills unpaid, either.

Which meant that no matter what she believed, she could be wrong. And one morning she might look in the mirror and the door to her memory would come flying open and she'd find herself in love with two men.

"Cara? Are you all right?"

The sound of Quinn's voice coming from just outside the open bathroom door startled her. She'd been so lost in thought she hadn't heard his approach. "I'm fine," she said. "You just scared me."

"But before that you were staring into the mirror with the damnedest frown I've ever seen. Are you still having a reaction from just looking at yourself? Or is your memory coming back?"

His own frown was pretty fierce, and to ease his mind she said, "Yes, weird things still happen in mirrors, but no, it isn't bringing my memory back, though it seems to be trying to." Then she turned to face him and teased, "You wouldn't be hoping for it so you can get rid of me, would you?"

He pretended to consider it, crossing his arms over his chest and leaning one shoulder against the door-jamb.

The black mock-turtleneck T-shirt he wore cupped every muscle like a caressing hand, but Cara tried not to notice how great it looked on him. Or how well his jeans fit, either.

He was looking her up and down in his teasing consideration, and his shining silver eyes shot heat that made her feel as if he could see right through her own sleeveless shirt and jeans.

Finally he said, "There are a lot of things I'd like to do with you, but get rid of you isn't one of them. In fact, if you weren't somebody else's bride . . ."

"Maybe you could borrow me," she flirted back, liking this man altogether too much.

His supple mouth stretched into a lazy grin. "Now there's an idea. And then if you gave me too much grief I could just return you."

Grief was not what she had in mind to give him. But what she said was "Forget it, then. It wouldn't be any fun if I had to worry about being on my best behavior all the time."

"And what have I been seeing so far? Your best behavior or you having fun?"

"I probably shouldn't admit this under the circumstances, but I've been having fun," she confirmed.

He nodded as if he'd known it all along. Then he pushed off the jamb and joked wryly, "Well, get your little rear in gear and I'll show you the time of your life."

Cara had no doubt he could.

If only he would.

SINCE CARA'S NEIGHBOR, Nancy Somers, had neither called nor returned any of the number of messages Quinn had left on her answering machine, the first stop they made in Arvada was to the apartment building.

Nancy Sommers was not there, and they had to settle for writing a note on the back of another of Quinn's business cards that asked yet again to speak to her, and slipping it under her door.

They also picked up Cara's mail—a discouraging past-due notice and a letter from the bank about insufficient funds.

Then they headed for the senior citizens' community to which Cara had written checks.

Springfield was set in a small, grassy area just off a road that looked as if it ran straight into the mountains.

Quinn pulled around the circular drive that curved in front of a one-story red-brick building and parked in a lot just beyond it. From there they could see several three-level buildings surrounding a tranquil lake complete with a small pier, park benches and a family of mallards being fed by a grandfatherly man.

"Nice place," Quinn commented as they rounded the car and set off across the lot to walk under a canopy and into the front building.

What they entered was a lobby that looked like an oversize entranceway in a well-decorated house. Quinn took a brochure from a round pedestal table in the center of the space and held it so Cara could read it at the same time he did. The pamphlet touted apartments where partially assisted living provided for the needs of the residents while still allowing them their independence.

Off the lobby were several meeting rooms, their doors open to a craft class in one, a lecture in another, a bridge game in a third and a slow-moving exercise group in the fourth. To the right of these was a dining room where only a few people were still eating lunch. To the left of it all was a closed door marked Director.

It was there that Quinn and Cara went. Quinn knocked, and from inside came, "Come in, come in, come in!"

Quinn opened the door and waited for Cara to go ahead of him.

Just as she did a man who was about her age looked up from where he sat working at a computer behind a desk. "Cara!" he greeted enthusiastically. "Welcome back from wherever you were on your mysterious getaway," he added with a laugh. "Your grandmother didn't tell me you'd gotten home. She must be thrilled, though. She's been so worried about you!" he said, standing to come around the desk.

He was an attractive man, though shorter and far slighter than Quinn. He had very red hair, blue eyes, deep dimples in each cheek and straight, white teeth that flashed in an easy smile that went along with the warm welcoming way about him.

Quinn stepped up and introduced himself, complete once again with business card and his account of Cara's amnesia.

"So it's my grandmother who lives here?" she asked when he'd finished.

"Tillie Warner," he supplied, staring at her as if she'd dropped from the ceiling. "I can't believe this," he added with a dumbfounded laugh.

"And you are...?" Quinn asked.

The director laughed yet again. "I'm sorry. I'm Grant Thompson. I run the place." He made a gesture intended to take in all of the Springfield community. Then he went on to ask several questions about Cara's health and what had happened to her.

"Tillie's been here since we opened six years ago," he informed them when Quinn got in a question of his own. "We all love her. She's such a spunky lady, so full of life and fun."

Cara could barely concentrate on what he was saying about this Tillie person as she waited for him to finish and launch into mention of bounced checks or payments due or past due.

When it didn't come she decided she had to ask.

But it only made him laugh again. "If only everyone was as conscientious as you are! You give Tillie a check every month like clockwork and she gives it to me. Usually with a bit of something chocolate that she's made herself to fatten me up."

"That's her grandmother, all right," Quinn muttered.

"And none of the checks have ever bounced?" she persisted.

"Never!" he answered as if it were too farfetched to even think such a thing about her.

Cara was relieved to finally hear there was one place where she wasn't in arrears.

"But I'm sure you don't want to stand around listening to me when Tillie can tell you anything you want to know," Grant Thompson said. "Besides, I couldn't, in good conscience, keep you here when she's been talking everyone's ears off wondering what might have happened to you." His smile turned flirtatious and he bent closer to her ear to add, "And telling me I might still have a chance with you since you didn't go through with the wedding." He wiggled his eyebrows in a way that left her unsure whether he was kidding or not.

"We'll need directions to the apartment," Quinn put in abruptly and in a voice loud enough to let the director know he wouldn't be ignored.

Cara glanced at him out of the corner of her eye, wondering about the sudden curtness in his tone.

But the redheaded man didn't seem to notice the change in Quinn's attitude. "I didn't think of that, but of course you will. Strange, strange, strange. It must be even more so for you," he said to Cara as he took out a map that showed an overview of the buildings.

She assured him her situation was unusual and would have looked at what he was explaining to her except Quinn stepped between them before she could.

"If there's anything else you need, don't hesitate to ask," the jovial man offered as Quinn thanked him flatly and took Cara's elbow in a possessive hold to steer her out of the office.

"Is something wrong?" she asked when they left the building and headed around the lake.

"Not a thing."

"You just didn't like Grant Thompson?"

"He's giddy." Quinn nearly spat the word.

"I'd describe him as happy. It's probably good for morale."

Quinn's head slowly pivoted her way, and when his gaze reached hers his eyes were steely. "Did something click for you with that guy?"

"You mean in my memory or are you referring to an attraction of some kind?" She could barely keep a straight face and knew she was being awful to tease him over what seemed to be a delicious show of jealousy.

But Quinn caught on because his tone turned dry and remote. "Was he familiar to you?" he reworded his question, as if that was all he'd meant in the first place.

"Nope. Cute, though. And personable."

"This grandmother of yours seems to think so, too, since she's doing some matchmaking. She must not think much of old Peter Whos-its."

"Don't change the subject."

"I didn't think I was."

"Bull! You were jealous of Grant Thompson and you know it, so you're trying to talk about Peter Whos-its instead," she said, laughing now.

"The director's just a pretty boy," he said with disapproval and dismissal all rolled into it.

"Wasn't he, though," she answered dreamily.

Quinn just glared at her as he held open the main door to the building just to the east of the lake. But all he said was "Here we are," in an ominous tone of voice.

Cara was enjoying herself but decided to let him off the hook as they reached the door to the apartment they'd been told belonged to Tillie Warner.

Quinn knocked and a high, lilting voice called, "Just a minute."

As they waited Cara considered her own feelings as she faced imminent contact with a member of her family. She had no image whatsoever of the woman inside the apartment, and yet she did have a sense of peace and gladness that she couldn't pinpoint an origin for, other than to assume she must be fond of Tillie Warner.

Then the door opened and both Cara and Quinn had to adjust their line of vision downward, for there, off to the side of the doorway, was a woman who looked like Mrs. Santa Claus in a wheelchair.

"Oh, my God! Cara! Finally!" she exclaimed, throwing her arms in the air for a moment before reaching for her and pulling her down into a big bear hug. "I've been waiting and waiting for you to at least call and let me know where you'd gone off to."

It felt natural to hug the fluffy little white-haired woman back so Cara did. Then Tillie let go of her and caught her hand to hold on to.

"There's something you need to know," Cara said as her grandmother's gaze went all the way up the long length of Quinn.

Cara introduced him, and for the first time he didn't make a move to produce a business card, but just smiled and said hello.

"Well, come on in, both of you. If you tell me what's going on out here, everybody'll hear and I won't get to retell it myself at pinochle tonight." She released Cara's hand then and wheeled herself into the living room of the tiny apartment that clearly accommodated her handicap.

Cara and Quinn followed her, closing the door behind them.

The living room, dining room and kitchen were all basically one open space. Everything in the kitchen—counters, cupboards, sink, appliances—was at a lowered height, and while there were three chairs at the table and a love seat in the living room, there was ample access for the wheelchair.

Cara thought the place looked a little like a child's playhouse, sparsely furnished and in a sort of miniature. But it was evident it allowed Tillie to take care of herself.

"You've nearly worried me silly," Tillie said as she maneuvered her chair to face the love seat and motioned for Cara and Quinn to sit there. "Not that I wasn't thrilled when you skipped out on that wedding at the last minute. You know how I felt about it and I was glad you didn't go through with it. But then, when I didn't hear from you—"

"No, I don't know how you felt about the wedding," Cara interrupted what seemed as if it could go on for some time. "I don't know much of anything."

Tillie looked at Cara, then at Quinn, then back at Cara. "What's going on?"

"I know this will sound crazy, but I..." She didn't want to alarm the old woman whose plump face was already creased with concern. So she ad-libbed. "Somewhere between my putting on my dress and actually getting to the wedding I bumped my head. I don't know how, but the next thing I knew I was in a meadow in the mountains, on property Quinn owns. He found me and I've been with him ever since. But the glitch is that I lost my memory along with several hours of this past Saturday."

Belatedly Cara wondered if a woman as old as Tillie would still have all her mental faculties and grasp what she'd just been told.

But the violet-colored eyes that matched her own seemed focused and alert. "Amnesia?" Tillie asked, astonished.

"I'm afraid so," Quinn confirmed, going on to assure her Cara was perfectly well and otherwise unharmed, and to fill in some of the details.

"Quinn is a private investigator," Cara added when he'd finished. "We've been tracking me down, and part of what we've found led us here."

"But you don't even know me, do you, babe?" Tillie caught on quickly.

"No, I don't. I mean, something about seeing you feels right. And good. But that's as far as it goes."

"Lord," Tillie breathed, rearing back in her chair and puffing out her ample chest.

"Maybe it would help if you could tell us a few things," Quinn suggested. "Beginning with the wedding and her fiancé."

"Peter Shelby," she said, making such an exaggerated grimace it looked comical.

"You don't like him?" Quinn asked.

"I liked his father," she offered as if to soften the truth. "But Peter is too much like his mother—Sheila the Shrew. She controls him, and he wants to control everything and everyone else." Tillie looked directly at Cara. "You mentioned that wedding dress but I don't suppose you remember that he bought it without so much as consulting you because he was afraid if you chose one yourself it wouldn't be good enough." She made a disgruntled humph deep in her throat. "If you'd have picked it out yourself it wouldn't have looked like something smuggled out of the French Revolution."

"I didn't like it much when I looked down and found myself wearing it," Cara admitted.

"Why did she accept it—the dress and the criticism?" Quinn asked.

"For the hotel," Tillie answered. "Though I don't know how she thought she could endure being married to him and his mother even for that."

"The hotel?" Cara prompted.

"The Rosegate."

"That old brownstone in downtown Denver that's near the new baseball field?" Quinn asked.

Tillie nodded. "It's also right in the middle of an area where renovations will turn several old warehouses nearby into extra convention facilities."

"I was marrying a jerk so I could get my hands on a hotel?" Cara asked in disbelief and distaste.

Tillie laughed. "Peter's a jerk, all right. But it wasn't as if you didn't have a right to the Rosegate."

"How so?" Quinn asked.

"Cara's father, Eddie, and Leo Shelby were friends from the time they were boys. Close friends. Like brothers. They went to school together, worked together, joined the army together, did everything together. They even got married only a few weeks apart. Eddie married my Mona and Leo married rooty-tooty Sheila, who always thought she was above everyone else because her father had a little money," Tillie explained to Quinn as if Cara already knew what she was talking about.

"After the weddings," the old woman went on, "Eddie and Leo were looking to go into a business of their own, so they borrowed money from Sheila's father to build the Rosegate. They made it a prestigious hotel to compete with the Brown Palace, the Fairmont and the Oxford in their heyday—the good places. And it did very well. Well enough to pay off Sheila's father and leave her no say in it, which made her mad, I can tell you. Over the years the hotel has suffered from age and location, but Eddie and Leo loved the place. And so does Cara," she said with a glance at her. "She loves it like a woman loves an only child. And she treats it that way, too, giving up her whole life to it."

Which Tillie's tone made clear she didn't approve of.

"Anyway," she continued, "some years back, as Cara and Peter got to marrying age—Peter is Leo and Sheila's son, who was born just two months before Cara—Leo and Eddie started thinking how much they'd like their two kids to marry each other. They tried putting them together, which wasn't hard to do since they both worked at the hotel, but Cara and Peter just didn't hit it off in that way. So Eddie and Leo made that damn will, like two feudal lords.''

"A will," Quinn repeated.

"It cut out the wives altogether and left the Rosegate to their kids. But with a big catch. If they marry they inherit the hotel. If they don't marry, each of them can work there, but for no more than a barely average wage while the hotel and all of its profits are held in trust until they turn fifty. And the executor of the trust, which is a legal firm, has complete decision-making powers over the hotel and its running.''

"So I agreed to marry this guy to inherit the hotel?" Cara reiterated, still finding it hard to believe until something else occurred to her, brightening her up considerably. "And then, once we had the place, we were going to get divorced, right?''

Tillie shook her head ominously. "If you divorce before you're fifty, it all reverts back to the trust until then.''

"What happens when they turn fifty?" This from Quinn.

"They inherit the place free and clear, as well as everything in the trust," Tillie addressed him again. "I tried to convince Cara to just wait for that. No hotel, no amount of money, is worth being tied for the next twenty years to a humorless man.''

"But Cara didn't want to do that," Quinn concluded. "Maybe she did have feelings for him.''

"No way," Tillie refuted with vigor. "But she said she didn't love anyone else and she'd made up her mind to do what she needed to do to inherit the Rosegate. She claimed she didn't take Peter's remarks and attitude to heart, that she could handle him and anything that came with him, and she wouldn't listen to any of my arguments.''

Tillie pointed a crooked finger at Quinn. "Now it might be different if she could have a little love in her life on the side. But there's even a stipulation in that damn will for an annual investigation to make sure they're both being faithful. Those two fools that called themselves fathers fixed it so their poor kids would turn to each other like the only survivors of a shipwreck—out of pure desperation and no other choice. Mona was so furious she even left Eddie for a while. She rented that apartment Cara's living in now. But nothing she said or did, nothing Sheila said or did, would make their husbands change it.''

Tillie's frustration was palpable in the room. "My Cara is too full of life to lock herself into a relationship with a stick like Peter Shelby and his obnoxious mother. She should have a husband to crawl into bed with every night and kids to run roughshod over in the day. What will happen when I'm not around anymore and the only family she's left with is Peter and Sheila? Why, they probably won't let her sit at the table with them for Thanksgiving dinner. They'll make her eat in the kitchen with the *staff*," she finished, giving full ridicule to the pretension of that last word.

Thinking of the message on the Shelby answering machine, Cara couldn't help smiling. She also couldn't help agreeing with everything the older woman said, though apparently it hadn't mattered before.

"Tell me about what led up to the wedding, the last time you and Cara talked and what you know about her disappearance," Quinn said.

"Not much of anything led up to it. Sheila had arranged for newspeople to come to the wedding itself so she'd get into the society pages again, but beyond that Cara wouldn't go along with any celebrations or parties or showers for what was a marriage of force.''

''Which explains why there was nothing on the calendar,'' Cara offered.

Tillie went on, again aiming her answer at Quinn, as if Cara remembered it all herself. ''As for the last time we talked, I was with her until just before the service was to start. It was in the ballroom of the hotel and she'd gotten ready in the dressing room down the corridor from it. One of the ushers came for me, and the last thing I said to her was, 'run for it while you still can.' When she didn't show up I thought she'd taken my advice and escaped out the delivery door.''

Tillie turned to Cara once more. ''Then, when I didn't hear from you and there was no answer at your apartment—and that stuffy old Peter would only put his nose in the air and say he didn't know where you were, either—well, I thought you must have just needed some time to yourself. But I was worried all the same.''

''Tell me about the delivery door,'' Quinn interjected.

Tillie looked back at him, though with an expression that said she thought the question was very strange. ''It's just a delivery door. There's one to the kitchen for food and liquor deliveries, and one near the ballroom so flower arrangements don't have to go through the heat of the kitchen.''

''How close to the dressing room is it?'' he persisted, drawing even more of a frown from Tillie.

''Very close. Right beside it.''

''Were there a lot of people milling around?''

"Not by the time they came for me. The corridor was empty. Why?"

"He's just wondering if I made my escape unobserved," Cara explained quickly, still hesitant to alarm the elderly woman, who was already obviously suspicious.

"Nobody I talked to saw you leave."

"And was everyone but you and Cara seated when you were taken in to the service?" Quinn asked.

"Everyone but me, Cara, Peter and Sheila. Peter and his mother were to have walked down the aisle after I was situated—she was giving him away, she said. But I sat there a good half hour before they finally showed up. Then no one could find Cara. It was a big fiasco." Tillie glanced at Cara. "How did you leave without your car?"

"I honestly don't know. My memory begins when I woke up in the meadow. I don't have a clue as to what happened to get me there." With the exception of getting shot, but that was what she didn't want the other woman to know.

"How did Cara get to the wedding without her car?"

"Limousine," Tillie answered with more of her comical exaggeration. "Sheila had us both picked up at home so the photographers could take pictures of us arriving in a long, white stretch limo as if we were movie stars attending a premiere. It was so silly. Cara must have called a cab and hightailed it out of there," she guessed in answer to her own question.

"We called the Shelby house," Cara said. "There was a message saying Peter and his mother had gone to Tulsa. And someone else we've run into said that was where I was supposed to be honeymooning. Did he really take his mother on the honeymoon?"

"*Honeymoon?* Ha! That was a business trip. There's a hotel-motel conference there this week. Sheila wanted to go all along. I suppose with you out of the picture she seized the day. She now has her hand in the Rosegate the way Leo would never let her when he was alive. She's always butting in, though she acts as if she's just helping Peter to repay him for supporting her."

"He has to support her?" Quinn asked.

"Between Leo leaving the hotel to Peter and her father going a little nutso and willing all of his estate to some fly-by-night church he got hooked up with at the end, Sheila was left without a cent."

There was a knock on Tillie's door just then that made her sit up straighter in her chair. "Damn! That's the van to take me to a doctor's appointment. If I cancel so we can talk more we'll still be charged," she said more in question than statement, as if wondering if Cara wanted her to do it, anyway.

"We wouldn't want you to miss seeing your doctor," Quinn said.

"Maybe we could drive you there?" Cara cast a glance at Quinn, hoping he wouldn't mind that she was volunteering him.

"Sure," he agreed. "We can tie the trunk lid over the chair."

But Tillie waved away the offer. "No, that's silly. The van is equipped for me to just roll on and off. For you two to do it would be a big hassle."

The elderly woman finally went to the door, where she told the driver she'd meet him in the parking lot, and then set about gathering her purse and keys as efficiently as anyone on two legs.

"I know you aren't staying at your apartment because I've called there at all hours of the day and night," Tillie told Cara as she and Quinn joined the elderly woman at the door. Then she did a verbal double take. "Do you even know about your apartment?"

"We tracked it down. But no, I'm not staying there. . . ." But how to explain why?

Quinn jumped in. "She'll be at my house for the time being," he said as if it didn't require more of an explanation than that.

"I know the apartment is already dismantled," Tillie allowed. "But the logical place for you to live until things get sorted out is here with me."

"Oh, I wouldn't want to put you out," Cara said in a hurry, realizing the moment the words were spoken how silly the formality sounded. This woman was her grandmother, her only family, and it was clear they were very close. Yet, not only would it not be safe for either of them, the woman was a stranger to her, more of a stranger than Quinn.

Once more he saved her. "It's better for Cara to be at my place for now."

Tillie's suspicions again materialized in her expression. She took a quick look at a clock on the wall of her kitchen, as if to see if she could spare the time to go into them.

"We'll walk you out," Quinn suggested before she could, and Cara took up the space at the back of the wheelchair to push Tillie, a gesture that somehow felt natural.

Then, along the way and before Tillie could ask any questions, Quinn gave her one of his business cards so she'd have his phone number, as if that sealed things.

Tillie took it and looked at it carefully. But she wasn't about to be deterred. She said pointedly to him,

"There's no reason Cara can't stay with me. She spends the night a lot—whenever one of us is lonesome or so we can have an all-night movie fest or for holidays. The love seat opens into the same kind of bed that's at her place, and that way I can look after her and fill her in on everything she's forgotten."

Cara saw Quinn give the old woman a smile and a wink. "Shh," he said confidentially. "I'm trying to keep her around as long as I can."

Tillie glanced from Quinn to Cara overhead, and back to Quinn, clearly still suspicious, but unable to resist the intimation of romance. "Think you can keep her from marrying that bozo if she changes her mind back and decides to do it again?"

His smile turned into a grin and he cast Cara a sideways look. "You never know."

The seniors' van was in front of the canopied entrance to the first building they'd gone into. The driver had a mechanical lift already lowered and awaiting Tillie and her chair. He took over for Cara and positioned the chair, but before Tillie would let him raise her into the van she caught Cara into another tight hug.

"Are you two sure everything is all right?" she demanded when she'd again released her.

Cara pointed her chin at Quinn. "I'm in good hands," she answered confidently.

"I really would like you to come stay with me."

"We'll be back and we'll keep you well informed," Quinn assured.

"Call me tonight or tomorrow," the old woman ordered as the driver finally got her into the van, locked the chair in place and took his own seat to start the engine.

"Don't worry," Cara called to her through an open window nearby.

Tillie made a face that said that was impossible, then settled her gaze on Quinn. "How about if you come and stay, too? We'll rent a fold-out—"

Quinn laughed lightly "I'll take good care of her."

"You better. I can be mean for an old lady in a wheelchair," she called as the van pulled away.

"Somehow, I doubt that," Cara said with a laugh.

"Oh, I don't know. I think she might do about anything for you. And you'd probably do about anything for her, including let rent on your own apartment slide to pay hers."

"I'm just glad there's one place I'm not in trouble over money," she said as she led the way off the curb into the parking lot.

She was vaguely aware of the noise of an engine revving up from somewhere nearby, but her thoughts were on all she'd just learned. She was still slightly in front of Quinn as they headed toward his car, when the sound of rubber burning against pavement screeched through the air.

Cara swung a glance over her shoulder at the same moment the spinning wheels caught to shoot a small gray sedan from out of nowhere.

Directly at her.

"Look out!"

Chapter Eight

The next thing Cara knew she was rolling on the grassy border of the entrance driveway with Quinn's hand a vise grip around her bare arm.

Then, all at once, an elderly couple ran to them and the director burst from the building.

"That car tried to run these folks over," the elderly man explained excitedly to Grant Thompson.

But Cara was only vaguely aware of what he was saying.

"Are you okay?" Quinn asked her, his body partly cushioning, partly protecting hers, his voice penetrating the confused haze she was in.

"I think so. Are you?" Things were coming together in her mind, and she realized he had grabbed her arm and yanked her along in a dive for the greenbelt that had taken them both out of harm's way.

"I'm all right," he answered, proving it by getting up and then helping her stand, too.

But the reality of what had happened was sinking in and her knees buckled under her.

Quinn caught her in a second show of quick reflexes, bringing her up against him.

Cara's heart was racing in her ears and her breathing was coming a little hard as a wave of pure fright rushed through her. Instinct made her cling to him as if he were the ballast in a storm, letting the power of his big body help settle her pulse, calm her breathing and return her sense of security.

"Shall we call for an ambulance?" Grant Thompson asked.

Reluctantly Cara straightened away from Quinn, though he still kept one arm around her, just in case. They both assured the director they didn't need medical attention.

Then Quinn turned to the elderly couple, including Grant peripherally. "Did anybody get the license number?" he asked, all business. "Or the make or model of the car?"

None of the three had. The only thing that could be established was that it had been a fairly new car with darkly tinted windows that completely obscured the driver from sight.

"It wasn't a car that I've seen before, I can tell you that," the subdued and serious Grant Thompson said. "It certainly didn't belong to one of our people."

"It could have been a visitor, though," the elderly woman suggested in a complaining tone. "Some of the young people who come by drive too fast through here."

Her husband clicked his tongue in impatience. "That car was aimed right at these folks," he insisted. "It charged them just like a bull charges a red cape, skidded out onto the street and disappeared around a curve. I saw it with my own eyes."

"Well, you can't see hardly a thing. Who was it couldn't even find the milk in the refrigerator this morning?"

"I think we better go in and call the police," Grant interrupted before the argument could go any further.

A small crowd had gathered by then and Cara saw Quinn's gaze scan it before he agreed with the director. "Go ahead and do that. I want to talk to these people in case one of them saw something." To Cara he said, "Sit down inside and take it easy. I won't be long."

With his arm still around her, he gave her shoulder one last squeeze before leaving her.

Cara watched his broad back for only a split second before it occurred to her that he was dispatching her to the geriatric set while he went off and had all the fun. And she might be shaken, but she wasn't ready for a rocking chair.

Ignoring the director's concerned calls, she went after Quinn.

"What are you doing, Cara?" he asked in an even voice.

"Just thought I should point out that that car could have been driven by somebody out to get you instead of me."

"Uh-huh," he said, clearly not believing it.

"Or that it's also possible the driver was just a lead-footed senior citizen feeling his oats in a borrowed car."

"Uh-huh." Still no belief.

"And I knew you wouldn't be able to concentrate on the interrogation if you were worrying about me being alone with Grant Thompson." The denouement was hard not to smile through.

"Not to mention that you couldn't resist playing P.I."

"That, too." But she could see him fighting a smile of his own and knew he didn't mind.

Several of the people looking on from the curbside knew Cara and were as interested in finding out what had happened at the wedding as they were in discussing the car that had nearly run her over. Of those who had seen anything, no one could offer information that helped, but they were still anxious to wait for the police so they could tell them the color of the car and its intent. All seemed to relish the role of witness.

Two police officers arrived just as that was becoming clear, and Quinn gave the chore over to the younger of the two, who was in line to hear more about grandchildren and personal scrapes with danger than about what had actually happened in the parking lot.

The other cop took statements from Quinn, Cara, the director and the elderly couple who had actually seen the most.

When they were finished with the on-site questions, the officer sent Cara and Quinn to the station to file a formal complaint.

A policewoman handled that chore and guided them through more paperwork before checking for prior incidents like this one, or reports of a gray sedan having been stolen. She didn't come up with anything and by the time Cara and Quinn were free to go, it was dark outside.

In the comfort of the passenger seat, Cara finally relaxed, glad to have this day coming to a close.

"So how was this for chills, thrills and excitement?" Quinn asked on the way home.

"Chasing down bad guys is more what I had in mind than dodging cars wanting to run over one of us. But it certainly gave me chills." She glanced at him in profile lit only by dash lights and the occasional glow of headlights from cars going in the opposite direction. His hair had fallen to his forehead when he'd tackled her, and even though she'd seen him finger comb it back, it still grazed his brow in a rakish way she liked very much.

"So," she went on, "do you think there's any chance this was a disgruntled husband you caught taking his secretary to the No-Tell Motel for a lunchtime tryst?"

He shook his head but didn't say anything, as if putting into words that she'd been the target might scare her.

"Well, I guess we've made progress, then," she said. "Somehow we've let whoever shot me in the first place know I'm back. In body if not in mind. Do you think they've been following us around waiting for the opportunity to strike again?"

He pointed a finger to his rearview mirror. "Nobody's been following us."

"So what does that mean? I ticked off some little old lady at Springfield who happened to see me today?"

Her joke didn't make him smile. "It could mean whoever is after you knows how close you are to Tillie and that sooner or later you'd show up there," he said seriously.

"I don't suppose anyone who knows me doesn't know I'm close to Tillie."

"That'd be my bet."

"So this doesn't tell us much, does it?"

"No. But Tillie did," he reminded as he pulled into his driveway.

"Aha!" she said as if he'd just revealed a discovery. "Then you do have someone who's moved to the top of the suspect list."

"Depends."

"On?"

"On when and if Peter Whos-its and his mother got back to hear your message on their machine."

"The plot thickens," she said melodramatically as they got out of the car and went into the house. "But what if they have an alibi?"

"Then we keep digging."

Quinn held the back door open for her and they went into the house. It felt good to be there, Cara realized. Safe. And it allowed her to shed the remnants of uneasiness that lingered behind the impression she wanted him to have that she was taking this in her stride.

"I don't know about you, but I'm starved," he said.

"Near misses make you hungry?"

"I think it has more to do with not having eaten since this morning. Aren't you?"

"Not very."

His look told her he knew the loss of her appetite had to do with the day's events, but he didn't say that. He only said, "It's hot and stuffy in here. How about if we open the windows and air it out while we take something to eat onto the patio?"

"Sure."

While he raided the refrigerator Cara opened windows. Then they took everything outside.

Ground lights surrounded the edges of the brick-paved area left open to the sky overhead, casting a warm white glow.

Cara and Quinn sat across from each other at a redwood picnic table. "Is Tillie a suspect?" Cara asked over the beer they were splitting.

Quinn laughed, a sound rich and deep that seemed to bounce off the house and wrap around her. "No. The bullet fired at you didn't come from someone that low to the ground. There's also the fact that she couldn't possibly have moved you, and she doesn't have a motive for hiring someone else to have done it. The opposite is true, actually. She depends on you. Besides," he added, "I liked her."

This time it was Cara who laughed. "And your liking someone precludes them from any wrongdoing?"

"I'm a pretty good judge of people," he said, his tone thick with insinuation that had nothing to do with what they were discussing. "I trusted you, didn't I?"

She held her glass up in toast to him. "And I'm forever grateful. Including for saving me today."

"I wouldn't want anything to happen to you," he said seriously, staring at her, his eyes penetrating, the expression sober on that handsome chiseled face.

There was always something sensual just beneath the surface when they were together, and the only thing that seemed to keep it at bay was trying to figure out the puzzle of her past.

But even then her awareness of him was heightened. Of the way his hand curved around his coffee mug or held a fork. Of the thickness of his wrist when he put on his sunglasses. Or the flex of his biceps when he opened a door for her, or the hardness of his thigh when he crossed one leg over the other. She even thought his feet were sexy when she came downstairs first thing in the morning and found them bare.

It was as if every detail fascinated her. Enthralled her. Turned her on.

And so when discussing her case wore itself out, the pure potency of her attraction to him rose like the pecans in a pecan pie.

Just the way it was now.

Cara tried to ignore it but she didn't have much luck. Instead she made an attempt to refuel the discussion of the day's revelations.

"I was glad to find out there's no emotional involvement between me and Peter Whos-its," she said. "I didn't think there could be, but it's nice to know. Freeing."

"I feel the same way," Quinn said, his voice deep, almost raspy. And much too sensual, though she didn't have the impression it was on purpose, but only his own reaction to the sweet scent of sensuality swirling around them.

"Did you think I was in love with him?" she asked.

"It seemed likely," he said.

"And what if we'd found out I was? Would you have been crushed?"

"Flat as a pancake."

"Me, too," she admitted very quietly and yet with a sultriness she hadn't known she was capable of. So much for the refueling.

"We still don't know the whole story, though," he cautioned. "Could be you haven't told Tillie everything. For instance, she doesn't seem to know about your money problems."

"True," she allowed. Her eyes strayed to his lips and her thoughts wandered from the subject at hand to what those lips felt like over hers. "Then again," she heard herself say, "maybe we know enough." A part of her couldn't believe she'd said that. What was she doing, trying to seduce him? Well, okay, so maybe she was.

He smiled at her with one side of that terrific mouth of his. But he didn't comment. And he didn't get up and come around the table, scoop her into his arms and carry her to bed the way she was wishing he would.

But he did lean forward and take one of her hands in both of his, rubbing feathery strokes along her wrist. "Has it occurred to you that you might be a virgin?" he asked, as if he knew exactly what was going on in her head.

"A virgin," she repeated, considering it. It seemed incompatible with the level of desire he could raise in her with just that voice of his licking its way down her spine the way it was right then. But without any memory, she conceded to the possibility. "I never thought about it, no. And the doctor who checked me out at the hospital that first night didn't really say, did he?"

"Only that you'd never given birth."

"So, what if I am a virgin?" She nearly whispered the challenge as he raised her arm and pressed a soft, warm kiss on the sensitive inside of her wrist.

"If you are, maybe you should be left that way."

Torture. The very suggestion was torture as he brushed her wrist with his tongue and left it to chill dry in a sensation that was very erotic. He had to be teasing. He *had* to be.

"Maybe I should be," she agreed, anyway, playing his game. Or at least what she hoped was a game.

He smiled that devil's smile of his. "Or maybe you shouldn't be."

She could only swallow back a groan of pleasure as he kissed his way farther up the inside of her arm.

When the table between them wouldn't let him go any higher, he stood and came around it. He propped one hip on the edge and pulled her to her feet to stand between his spread thighs, letting just the heels of his hands run up her bare arms so lightly it erupted goose bumps in its wake.

With him half sitting, they were eye to eye and the soft white light around them seemed to dance in his. Cara did what she'd been wanting to all evening—she smoothed his hair from his brow. Not because she didn't like the way it looked. She did. But it was the closest she could come at that moment to running her fingers through it.

The shirt she wore was V-necked, and he found a spot at the base of her throat to kiss, making sparks skitter all along her nerve endings. She raised her chin and closed her eyes, reveling in the feel of his lips, of his warm breath against her skin, of his hands resting lightly on her waist, of just being so near to him, touched by him.

She gave in to the urge to learn the contours of his arms with her palms, riding the bulges to his well-defined biceps as he kissed the side of her neck, her collarbone, the peak of her shoulder...

But he stopped suddenly and she felt him draw back.

Opening her eyes, she found him studying her arm where there was a bruise dark enough to be seen even in the dim light, the spot where his hand had been when he'd pulled her to safety.

But that fact didn't seem to lessen his being appalled. "I hurt you," he said in a husky voice.

"I didn't notice it," she assured, far more intent on what was happening at that moment than anything that had happened earlier.

"What about now?" he persisted as he ran a gentle finger over it.

The bruise was sore enough for even that to register pain. But Cara said, "It's fine."

He must not have believed her because he kissed her there with such tender care that she half expected the discoloration to magically disappear.

Of course it didn't. But the magic stayed just the same. It was there in what was passing between them, in the reality that what they'd denied themselves before could finally come to be.

He straightened and cupped her face in both hands to cover her mouth with his. Gently and at his leisure, it was almost as if he was intent on teaching her, on showing a novice how good it could be.

But Cara didn't need instruction. Everything was alive inside of her, wanting him, craving him, crying out for him in a way that seemed natural, instinctive, leaving memory unnecessary.

Then he abandoned her mouth and again she opened her eyes to see why. This time he was staring fiercely down at her from beneath a serious frown. "I'm falling in love with you," he said as if he wasn't altogether happy about it.

But Cara understood. The future was ambiguous. And he was once again breaking his own rules. "I'm falling in love with you, too," she whispered from her heart.

Still, he seemed to hesitate, to weigh if they should really go on. But in the end he said, "Tonight is all that matters."

He took her hand again, this time to lead her through the house and upstairs to his room, where moonlight christened his big bed.

"Take off your shoes but leave the rest for me," he ordered as he kicked his own into a corner and crossed his arms over his middle to roll his T-shirt off over his head.

Lord, how long she'd wanted to see him without a shirt!

And suddenly there he was, standing just inside the moon glow.

Perfect. He was magnificently, masculinely perfect. She'd imagined what he looked like a hundred times, but not once had she done him justice. Honed muscle and hard bone, as finely drawn as a Michelangelo sketch, he was the image of power encased in smooth, taut flesh.

More than anything she wanted to touch him and she used stepping away from her shoes and socks as an excuse to put herself even just a little nearer to that goal.

Quinn met her halfway, wrapping her in his arms. She slipped hers around him, lying her flattened palms on his broad, naked back, and her cheek against those magnificent pectorals. His skin was as sleek as it looked, as warm, as tight, and she absorbed it all as if he were the sun taking away a chill.

But he wanted more than that and he proved it by cupping her face to raise it again to his open mouth and his seeking, probing tongue in a fresh hunger as he reached for the buttons of her blouse.

Anticipation soared inside her all over again. It wasn't possible for him to unfasten them quickly enough to suit her, to free her to feel his hands, his body against her own flesh.

But he was a terrible tease. He undid those buttons so slowly it was as if he'd never done it before. And each lazy movement, each scant brushing of his wrists against her straining nipples hidden inside the fabric, only mounted her desire for him.

Then, finally, he took off her shirt and bra, pulling her against the broad expanse of his glorious chest a second time.

He moaned softly at that first contact, mingling his breath with hers as the kiss turned instantly hungrier, more urgent, more uninhibited.

Not that Cara felt many inhibitions. Whether it was just a matter of her feelings for Quinn or a fact of her nature, she didn't know, or really care, as she kissed him back with a wild abandon, meeting and matching his tongue thrust for thrust.

His hands were splayed against her bare back when they began a slow massage that drew them upward to knead her shoulders, to delve deeply into the tendons, working any small bit of tension out of her. Then he made his way to her sides and around to fill his palms with her breasts, claiming them.

This time it was Cara who moaned as those giant hands encompassed her sensitive flesh to drive her insane.

And then they dropped to the waistband of her jeans.

She was ready to be completely naked before him. Anxious to be. As ready, as anxious, as she was for him to be naked before her. She found the snap and zipper that constrained him, too, and went to work on them, surprised to find her hands shaking just a little.

He smoothed her jeans down by sliding his palms from the small of her back to her derriere, and it felt so good she did the same to him, until finally they were rid of all the barriers between them.

As if he'd seen her earlier fantasy, he swung her up into his arms and set her on the bed. But he didn't join her there immediately. For a moment he stood staring down at her just as she stared at him, and in that instant she somehow knew she'd never wanted anyone as much as she did Quinn.

Then he came to her, working his wonders at her breasts with hands and mouth, tongue and even teeth, until her back arched off the mattress in answer to him kissing her, caressing her, loving her.

He seemed to know her every wish, her every desire, meeting them all and each time raising an even greater need in her to feel him inside of her, filling her, completing her.

Just when it was so intense she thought she couldn't possibly wait any longer, he parted her thighs with his knee and rose above her, bracing himself on outstretched arms on either side of her head. He was the image of pure power poised for one brief moment before finding his home in her with as much care as any virgin could ask for, until they were joined fully, deeply, wonderfully.

If she'd ever before experienced the poignant ecstasy of finally being united with the man she loved, she didn't remember it, and so what swept through her at that first melding of his body with hers was overwhelming. Joyous tears rushed to her eyes and she held him to her, wanting the moment to last forever.

He kissed her hair, her temples, her nose. And then his mouth met hers once more in a kiss that sealed it all with tenderness.

But passion wouldn't be ignored and lips parted with a will of their own, tongues played again, and below, just one pulse of that long, hard shaft sent a bolt of lightning through Cara that started everything singing again.

And then he began to move. Thrusting slowly, slowly, in and out, each stroke embedding him all the way to the core of her, again and again, like the first turns of a train's wheels, building speed, building intensity, until they were racing together, faster, harder, through passion to glorious explosive ecstasy that made Cara cry out, holding on to Quinn, never wanting it to end. Never! Never....

But even as she crossed over the peak and the ebb began, the sensations were blissful, made more so when she found Quinn just reaching his climax, his steely body taut, a low, primitive moan of release sounding in his throat as he drove into her, sending ripples of her own pleasure repeating itself as he, too, reached the crest.

His momentum spent, he slowed back to the pace that had started it all, winding down until they both lay still.

Quinn's breath came hard and fast in her ear and their bodies met so perfectly it really was as if they were just one, fitted together the way they were meant to be. Too perfectly to part, and so, holding her close, he rolled them to their sides.

He stroked her hair. He kissed the top of her head, staying there to whisper in a deep, raspy voice, "I love you."

She wanted to tell him she loved him, too, because her heart was brimming with it. But her head had found its niche in the crook of his neck and shoulder, and she was too tired to speak. She could only manage a soft, replete sigh before sleep dragged her near.

But she knew he knew.

Because an act as wondrous as what they'd just shared could come from nothing less.

QUINN WAS ON his back and Cara was lying against his side, her head on his shoulder, when the phone rang and woke him with a jolt. He had no desire to disturb the arrangement so he considered not answering it.

But by the third ring he'd thought of all the reasons he had to and reached only one arm to the nightstand to pick it up, bringing the receiver to his ear without moving anything else.

"Is this Quinn Strummel?" the caller asked.

"Hi, Tillie," he answered very quietly, recognizing the old woman's voice and wondering what time it was.

"You sound like I woke you up. It's only nine-thirty. Do you go to bed that early?"

"Busy day," he said with a smile and a glance down at Cara, who barely stirred.

"I don't know how busy it was but I just got back from pinochle, where I heard about you and Cara nearly getting run over. And I want to know what's going on. Is my Cara in some sort of danger? No, never mind, don't bother to answer that because I know you're going to say she isn't and I'm not going to believe it. A person gets older and people treat her like a child again."

But he answered her honestly. "It's possible Cara could be in some danger. That's why I'm keeping her with me." He'd gone along with Cara when she'd downplayed what had happened to her because, after all, Tillie was her grandmother. But now he didn't think he was telling the elderly woman anything she hadn't already guessed. Tillie was no fool. Besides, in his experience people dealt better with what they knew than with what they imagined.

"She didn't just fall and hit her head before the wedding, either, did she?"

"No, she didn't. But I'm not going to let anything else happen to her." His arm tightened around Cara in reflex. He was glad when Tillie didn't ask exactly what had happened to her granddaughter because he wasn't sure he'd go so far as to tell her she'd been shot.

"Well, I've been thinking about some things since I heard about that car. Things that didn't matter when I was going along with the malarkey she tried to feed me today. But they might matter if somebody's out to get her."

This was another part of the reason he didn't usually keep things from people. When they knew the truth, it was possible something that hadn't seemed important before would occur to them. Something vital.

"Go ahead. I'm listening," he told her.

"Peter and Cara had an argument the night before the wedding. A big one. Cara had found out that once they inherited the Rosegate Peter had secret plans to change it completely. He was going to turn it into something not much better than a motel. There was no way Cara would stand for that. She wanted to do some remodeling, spruce it up, modernize a little, but retain its old-fashioned charm and dignity. But Peter wanted to fire the chef and turn the restaurant into a cut-rate coffee shop, and use one of the banquet rooms for a video arcade, and cut services, and a whole slew of other things that raised the hairs on the back of Cara's neck. She let him know in no uncertain terms that she wouldn't go along with it."

"Peter couldn't have liked that."

"He said she was too ignorant to see that they could make so much more money his way. Cara told me she was sure she could fight it. That once the hotel and the trust were released to them, Peter would have plenty of cash and listen to reason. But I don't know about that. I can't see Peter or Sheila ever thinking they have enough money."

"But was this something either of them might hurt her over?"

Tillie sighed. "Well, we can't ever really be sure what anybody will or won't do, can we? But what I've been worrying about is what that damn will provides for if something happens to Cara."

Tillie's body might not work the way it should, but there was nothing wrong with her mind. Quinn had been wondering the same thing since learning there was a will. "I intend to find out," he told her.

"In the meantime, don't let Cara out of your sight."

"That's my plan."

The little old woman's voice softened and he could tell it suddenly came through a fear-tightened throat. "She's all I have in the world. I'd sooner die myself than lose her," she said in such a hushed voice it was nearly a prayer. "Don't let anything happen to her."

It was on the tip of his tongue to tell her he'd sooner die than lose Cara, too, but he didn't say it. Instead he did all he could to assure Tillie everything would be fine before finally hanging up.

The steady, even sound of Cara's breathing let him know she was still asleep and for a time he just listened to it.

What he'd said to her grandmother had not been empty reassurances. He'd meant every word. Because he loved Cara in a way he'd never loved anyone before. In just the short time since he'd discovered her in that meadow she'd become a part of him.

A part that might not be easy to hang on to, he admitted to himself.

He didn't doubt his ability to keep her safe. But until they met up with her fiancé and heard what old Peter Whos-its had to say, he wouldn't feel as if they had the whole picture. And without the whole picture he couldn't be sure exactly what he was up against.

He knew one thing, though. Old Peter Whos-its didn't have any idea what he was up against, either.

Cara may have come into Quinn's life on a fluke, but now that she was there, he wasn't letting her go without a fight, that was for damn sure.

Beside him, she sighed and moved slightly, raising her thigh over his and snuggling closer to him in a way that pressed her breasts to his rib cage and brought the warm juncture of her legs to ride his hip.

That was all it took to turn his thoughts from fighting to something far more pleasant. More pleasurable. And he decided he'd take care of tomorrow when tomorrow came.

For now, he had her in his bed, in his arms, and he was going to make the most of it.

He was going to do what a ringing telephone and a conversation hadn't been able to.

He was going to wake Cara and put this night to good use one more time.

At least.

Chapter Nine

He slept on his back, absolutely still, his handsome face at perfect repose. His eyelids didn't twitch, his lips were closed, he didn't even snore. And if Cara hadn't been near enough to hear each deep inhale and exhale of breath she might have wondered if he were real.

But she was near enough. She was lying on her stomach, her chin atop two pillows that were over his outstretched arm—the one that had been wrapped around her when they'd fallen asleep just before dawn. Her side ran the length of his, one of her legs was casually, comfortably, familiarly resting over one of his and she'd been watching him sleep for about a half hour.

It must be love, she thought, amused at herself, for what else could content a person with watching another person sleep?

And she was content. More than content. She was enjoying just the rhythm of his breathing, studying the night's growth of his heavy, dark beard, learning the way his hair fell boyishly to his brow after hours of lovemaking, realizing for the first time what long, thick eyelashes he had—lashes any woman would sell a limb for.

The mighty Quinn, whose size and the pure power of his masculinity made his long eyelashes beyond notice. Just the way that size and masculinity camouflaged the softer side of him that she knew he didn't show to many people. But she'd seen it. And she'd heard it in the words he whispered as he made love to her. Felt it in his touch. It made her feel all the more special to be one of a chosen few.

Lord, but she loved this man!

"Let me guess," he said then, opening his eyes only slightly. "You're practicing surveillance."

"I'm pretty good at it, too," she joked back. "I'm also happy to report that I am not the only one apt to oversleep. It's past noon and here you are."

"Hard night with an insatiable woman," he muttered.

"As I recall, it was *you* who kept waking *me* up."

"And as I recall, there weren't any complaints."

Cara smiled.

"Tell me it isn't really that late," he said.

She nodded toward the clock on his nightstand. "Twelve-fourteen."

"Damn."

"Did you have somewhere you needed to go?"

In answer he moved the thigh she had her leg over so that it came up against that portion of her body that had given them both so much pleasure during the night. But after just a moment he took it away again. "As much as I'd like to spend the whole day in bed with you, we have work to do."

Cara knew the work involved seeking out her fiancé. She was not anxious to get to it.

She raised her thigh until it covered that long, hard shaft she'd come to know so well. "Are you sure?"

He curled the arm she was lying on to brush the backs of his fingers against her temple. "I'm sure I could spend a couple of days here making love to you."

"Only a couple?"

He opened his hand and slipped his fingers through her hair to cup the back of her head, massaging her scalp, rubbing sensuous circles at her nape with his thumb to set off fresh sparks.

But when he went on speaking, his words denied what he was starting up between them. "I'm also sure that whoever shot you is trying to finish the job, and we need to figure out who that is before they can surprise us with the next attempt." He arched up off the mattress to kiss her head and then slipped his arm from under her and got out of bed. "So we need to get going," he said, leaving the matter closed and Cara to groan her disappointment.

There was a consolation, though—Quinn's bare backside as he headed for the bathroom.

She watched him the whole way, sighing to herself in a reluctant acceptance but still wishing for him back in bed where life was definitely more simple than it would be beyond it.

TILLIE HAD BEEN RIGHT about the construction going on all around the Rosegate. Cara and Quinn drove through activity the likes of which that area hadn't seen in years, Quinn explained.

The Rosegate itself stood alone on a full city block, a stately twelve-story brownstone with cobalt-blue awnings over the entrance and windows on the first floor adding warmth and an inviting ambience.

The minute Cara set eyes on the place she had the same sense of familiarity and fondness she'd had with Tillie, though no actual memories came to her.

Inside, friendly greetings from people who seemed strangers to her welcomed her from all around. She could hardly stop and explain that she didn't remember them, so she merely answered their hellos as she and Quinn made their way through the red-velvet-adorned lobby to the front desk, where a young man had watched their progression with a forced smile on his very thin face and twice glanced furtively over his shoulder at the door behind him marked Management.

"Cara," he said tentatively when they reached him, smiling uncomfortably. "Mr. Shelby will be...*interested* to know you're back."

"Is he here?" Quinn asked while Cara was still trying to decide whether or not to bluff her way through this or explain her condition.

The desk clerk's eyes shot to Quinn and then away as if he didn't want to commit to full eye contact. "He's been here since early this morning. Mr. Shelby *and* Mrs. Shelby. And they aren't in good moods," he answered, ending with a confidential tone of voice that was aimed at Cara at the same time he nodded slightly over his shoulder.

"We'll just go on back, then," Quinn said, taking Cara's arm to lead her around the desk and through the door.

The first thing she saw in the hallway beyond was her own name on an old oak door to the right. She had the urge to go into the office that was clearly hers, though there was no real reason for it, beyond the feeling that it offered an escape. An escape she was longing for at that moment.

But that wasn't where Quinn took her. Instead he turned to the identical door facing it.

Peter Shelby's name was there.

Seeing that other door, that name printed out in block letters right in front of her face, sent a wave of the same sense of dread she had when she looked in mirrors. So strong was it that it flashed through her mind to tell Quinn she wanted to leave. Right then. No matter what.

But before she could say anything, he knocked on the door.

Her heart started to pound and the ringing in her ears began again, like an alarm. Was it her subconscious telling her that Peter Shelby was the one who had shot her? she wondered. Or was it just that she so desperately didn't want this part of her past back?

The woman who opened the door was taller than Cara and had a boxy body in an impeccable red suit. Her hair was golden, her elaborate makeup so flawless it looked natural, and the expression that was initially imperial turned scornful when her hazel eyes registered Cara.

She huffed once and then sneered. "Is this the grand reappearance?"

Before Cara or Quinn answered, an even more disdainful male voice sounded from behind the woman, who had to be Sheila Shelby. "Oh, don't tell me, Cara's back."

Sheila swung away from the doorway and there stood her counterpart—tall, lean, blond, attractive, well dressed and so disgusted he looked as if he wanted to spit on Cara. No doubt this was Peter Shelby. His sneer matched his mother's, too. "Did you have a nice little getaway?" he said sarcastically.

Cara looked at Quinn, whose dislike of these two was nearly palpable, and said pleasantly, "Is there any chance they *aren't* Peter and Sheila Shelby?"

Sheila did a dramatic turn from the door and crossed the room to a chair next to the desk inside. Each step announced her anger, even on the carpeted floor. She sat like a queen on a throne, waiting for entertainment she was sure not to like.

"I suppose you'd better come in," Peter said ungraciously, stepping out of the way to allow it and then shutting the door with just enough force to let it be known he'd have slammed it were he not such a cultured person.

"There's something you need to know right off the bat," Quinn began in his best authoritative tone. But he didn't get any further than that.

"You must be the bogus detective Nancy told us about. The backup for that idiotic amnesia story," Peter said with as much contempt for Quinn as for Cara.

Quinn turned a slow glance to Cara and gave her a look of mock indignation. "*Bogus* detective," he muttered deadpan.

"*Idiotic* amnesia," she muttered the same way, raising her eyebrows in exaggerated surprise that mirrored his ridicule of these two.

"Oh, very cute," Peter Shelby ground out. "You leave me at the altar to face two hundred guests, disappear without a word and then show up with this..."

"Bogus detective," Quinn supplied amiably.

Peter ignored him. "Acting all wide-eyed and innocent, as if you didn't completely humiliate Mother and
me, and your own grandmother, for that matter."

"Calm down, Petey. Remember your ulcer."

Facing this mother-son act of overdrawn indignation dispelled all of Cara's initial dread. They seemed
too ludicrously snobbish to take seriously. Or to be
frightened of, though she knew that shouldn't be any
reassurance.

Peter rounded the desk and sat in the oversize chair
behind it, looking too much like a child in his father's
seat.

Quinn crossed his arms over his chest and shifted his
weight to one hip. Then he poked his chin in the direction of the telephone. "Call Lutheran Hospital's
emergency room. They can verify Cara's amnesia. It's
a result of the side of her head being grazed by a bullet
some time just after her grandmother left her to be
seated for the service."

"That's absurd," Sheila said quickly.

"Call the hospital," Quinn repeated. "Or the police. There'll be a full report with the Wheat Ridge department and the Denver one, too."

Peter and Sheila exchanged a glance but neither of
them reached for the phone.

After a moment Sheila stared at Cara. "Who shot
you?" she demanded, still dubious but apparently
conceding to the possibility that there was some truth
to it.

"We're piecing that together," Quinn said. "That's
why we'll need some questions answered."

"You don't think one of us did it?" Peter demanded.

Quinn didn't respond to that. Instead he said, "For starters, when did the two of you get back from Tulsa?"

"What difference does that make?" This from Peter again.

Quinn just waited, staring calmly at them until Sheila finally said, "Early yesterday morning," as if it were inconsequential.

"And how did you spend the rest of the day?"

"What could that possibly have to do with Cara getting shot and not going through with the wedding?" Peter reiterated, putting more emphasis on the crime of missing the wedding.

Sheila stretched a long arm over the corner of the desk and patted her son's hand. "There's nothing to be done about the wedding now," she said in a sudden change of attitude. "If someone shot Cara, it wasn't in her control and the best thing we can all do now is sort through it so we can go on." Then she turned a newly composed and falsely friendly expression back to Cara and Quinn. "Peter and I just piddled around yesterday. We ran a few errands, unpacked, things like that."

"Did you run the errands together?"

"Some of them. Some of them we went our own ways to do," Sheila said. "But I agree with Peter. What does yesterday have to do with anything if this whole thing happened just before the wedding?"

Again Quinn disregarded the question to go on with his own. "The Nancy you mentioned—would that be Nancy Sommers?"

"Did you talk to any other Nancys?" Peter snapped snidely. "Of course it was Nancy Sommers."

"So she isn't just Cara's neighbor. How do you know her?"

"Don't go bringing Nancy into this. I won't stand for that," Peter said, even higher on his horse, if that was possible.

This time even Sheila ignored him and answered Quinn's question. "Nancy's mother was my best friend. Nancy and Peter practically grew up together, and we've all remained close—maybe even closer— since her mother passed away last year. I consider Nancy the daughter I never had."

Quinn turned his gaze on Peter. "How about you? Are you and Nancy Sommers *close?*"

For a moment Cara thought steam might actually come out of Peter's ears. "Nancy is a beautiful, warm, kind, wonderful person. Beyond reproach. And I will not discuss her with the likes of you."

"I'll take that as a yes," Quinn muttered. Then he said, "Is she also friends with Cara?"

"Well, they're friendly," Sheila answered. "It isn't as if they lunch together, but Cara did tell Nancy of the vacancy in her apartment building when Nancy was looking for a new place. She also gave Nancy a good reference so they'd rent to her. Does that matter, too?" Sheila asked, showing impatience. Then, as if she knew she wasn't going to get an answer, she looked at Cara and said with renewed disbelief, "Do you honestly not remember any of this?"

Cara shrugged. "Not a thing. Not even my own grandmother. We had to track her down."

"Then maybe you don't remember how important it is for us to get married," Peter said.

"I don't remember that either, no. But Tillie did explain some things about the will."

"Why don't you fill us in?" Quinn suggested.

"This is a nightmare," Peter grumbled before explaining. "It's absolutely imperative that we marry—both for you and for mother and I. We've had to second mortgage our home, give up mother's Jaguar, even sell some of her jewelry to pay the staff. We just cannot survive on a paltry manager's salary. To be blunt, we're going broke at the same time we're sitting on a small fortune we can't touch and a hotel that could be turned into a gold mine."

"That's why it's absolutely imperative for you. Why is it absolutely imperative for Cara?" Quinn asked.

"Because of Tillie, of course," Sheila said.

"Tell us about Tillie," Cara invited. "Why is she in a wheelchair?"

"Crippling arthritis complicated by a small stroke she suffered several years ago that left her unable to walk," Sheila explained with too much compassion. "The poor woman has had a hideous five years. She had the stroke at about the same time the pension fund from the steel company where she was a secretary her whole life was embezzled. Suddenly she was reduced to nothing but her Social Security benefits to live. That wouldn't have been enough even if she'd been in good health. But as it was, well, it would afford her only a bed in one of the low-quality nursing homes. I assume you've seen Tillie?" Sheila asked Cara.

"Yesterday."

"Then you know she's sharp as a tack and not at all sickly in spite of her handicaps. She needs some professional care and help getting through her day—help your parents couldn't give—but it would also have been cruel to put her in a home. Springfield was the perfect solution. Its specialized accommodations are costly, but your parents were subsidizing it when they were killed in the same car accident that took Leo.''

"Mother would have been killed, too," Peter added with a visible shudder. "Only a sudden headache kept her from being with them that night going to dinner.''

"But that was when all our problems started," Sheila continued. "I had no idea that both Leo and Eddie had cashed in their life-insurance policies and put the money into the hotel. Again. They both left nothing but the Rosegate and they'd tied it up in that hideous will."

"And Tillie was left a second time without enough money to live," Quinn said to prompt her back to the subject.

"Cara took over. She and Tillie have always been like this—" Sheila held up two crossed fingers. "You'd think they were girlfriends instead of grandmother and granddaughter. Cara couldn't care for Tillie herself any more than her parents had been able to, but she wouldn't see her moved out of Springfield, either. It was a strain on her parents' finances but Eddie and Leo took a better living from the hotel than the managers' salaries they left their children to. As difficult as it may be to believe, Cara has struggled even more than Peter and I."

"That is difficult to believe," Quinn murmured.

"And then it got worse." Peter took up the story with a sharp edge to his voice for Quinn's remark. "Tillie's arthritis is progressive and she's had to begin taking an extremely expensive medicine that her health insurance will pay only a small portion of. She has no supplemental coverage, and so within the past year Cara has had to pay the difference on everything, as well as absorbing increases in Tillie's rent." He looked at Cara once more. "The bottom line here is this—without the inheritance, either Tillie is going to end up in a nursing home after all or you're going to have to live in that rattletrap of a car because you can't keep two households going and pay for Tillie's medical needs. So you agreed with mother and I that we *had* to marry."

"No, no, don't bother trying to sweep me off my feet," Cara joked.

Sheila and Peter both stared at her as if she'd said something in a foreign language neither of them understood.

"Tillie didn't say anything about this," Quinn said.

"Tillie doesn't know that Cara can't afford all she's been doing," Peter explained. "Cara has protected her from it. Tillie knows her manager's salary is not great, but Cara has made sure she doesn't know she's a hardship or that Cara is in serious financial trouble." He focused on Cara suddenly, as if Quinn had left the room. "Our marrying is the only solution for us all. I've raised the Rosegate's revenues since we took over—"

"Single-handedly?" Quinn cut in. "While Cara sat across the hall and ate bonbons?"

Peter ignored him. "There's plenty of money in the trust to get both of our heads above water and remodel to accommodate the changes in this area."

This time it was Cara who interrupted him. "Yes, what about the remodeling you have in mind? Tillie tells us I didn't agree with it."

"Oh, she's just an old woman, what does she know?" Sheila said cattily, the words slipping out from behind that sympathetic demeanor she'd adopted in telling Tillie's history.

"Modernizing is an absolute must," Peter decreed.

"But to what extent?" Cara persisted.

"To the extent that's necessary," Peter said, looking down his nose. "We need to bring in people with children so we can cash in on them. We need to cut costs, cut serving time in the restaurant to run more people through and—"

"Sounds like Tillie had it right," Quinn broke in.

"You want to take away the amenities, the dignity, the charm," Cara added.

"Don't start that ignorant sentimental garbage again. I want to make money," Peter said, his avarice showing. Then he went on as if playing the ace he held. "And you need it every bit as much as we do or that precious grandmother of yours is going to end up just where you don't want her to be."

Cara looked at Quinn and said, "He is irresistible."

"Now, Cara," Sheila soothed, clearly wanting to smooth the waters her son had rippled, "you must understand what poor Peter has been through. He's—we're both—distraught with worry over money. And so are you, when you're in your right mind. Then we were both mortified when you didn't show up for the ceremony. Peter was up all night long with his stomach in knots over it. Just when we thought a solution was at hand, you seemed to snatch it away and the horrible worry began all over again. Peter is at wit's end. As were you, if only you could recall. Forgive him for the results of his despair."

Cara had the urge to make some sort of religious gesture. She fought it as Sheila went on.

"Ordinarily the two of you get along very well. You may not be romantically involved, but I don't think I'm mistaken in saying that you share a sibling sort of affection for one another that will surely serve you both in beating that wretched will.''

Peter took his mother's lead, apologizing. Then he said, ''I don't suppose you remember this, either, but we had plans to contest the terms of the will when we'd inherited the money and could afford the legal representation to do it. There's a fair chance we can get the courts to throw it out, divorce and go on with our lives. But we have to marry to get the money first because neither of us can even begin to afford what it will cost.''

Contesting the will was the only good idea she'd heard yet. In fact, it struck her as a very good idea. ''What's a 'fair chance'?''

''The attorney says he's fifty percent sure we'll succeed.''

''That's not a fair chance, that's only half a chance,'' Cara pointed out.

''Well it's better than nothing, isn't it?'' Peter shouted.

She had to concede to that. ''How long would it take?''

''Probably two years. But just think, Cara,'' Peter said, suddenly sounding like a man with gold fever, ''the sooner we go through with the wedding and get the suit under way to have the will thrown out, the sooner we could have our rightful inheritance and be free, too. The sooner we could both have a normal life, marry people we care about, have families of our own.''

''Or a court could rule to uphold the will and you'd have to stay faithfully married for twenty or so more years,'' Quinn said.

The look Peter shot him was ugly before he turned back to Cara. ''But either way we'd have the inheritance, the hotel. Mother and I could go on living the way we need to be happy, and you could afford to keep Tillie and yourself both comfortable.''

He opened his drawer and took out a business card, holding it out to Cara. ''Call the attorney, talk to him if you want. He convinced you before that this was worth a try. Let him do it again.''

Cara took the card, glanced at it and slipped it into her pocket.

''I have a few more questions,'' Quinn said, obviously approaching the end of this meeting.

Sheila and Peter glared at him as though they wished he'd just go away and mind his own business.

''What kind of car does Nancy Sommers drive?''

The mention of that name once again ignited protective outrage in Peter. ''Is this some sort of game you're playing?''

Quinn merely stared at him levelly, waiting.

Finally Peter said, ''She drives a green compact.''

''And would she be the person you'd marry if you were free of the will's stipulations?''

''That's none of your business,'' Peter snapped.

Quinn nodded slowly, clearly making an assumption but not pressing the matter. ''Tillie tells us the two of you were late for the wedding. Why was that?''

Peter looked at his mother out of the corner of his eye as if he didn't know how to answer that.

''I'm afraid that was my fault,'' Sheila said. ''My hairdresser simply could not get my hair to do what I wanted.''

Again the nod, this one noncommittal.

''Okay. Just one more question. What does the will provide for in the event of Cara's untimely death?''

Sheila's eyes narrowed to unflattering slits.

Peter's expression grew even tighter, angrier. "You are insinuating something!"

"Just asking questions. Part of the job."

"The will provides for the same thing if *either* of us dies without having children of our own to inherit the Rosegate," Peter rasped. "The other one of us immediately inherits it all."

Quinn's third nod seemed to say this was just what he suspected.

Peter took offense. To Cara he said, "Who does this guy think he is, anyway?"

"He's the man who's helping me sort through things," she informed evenly. "I have no doubt he's the man who will find out who shot me and get whoever it is off the streets."

"Well, don't let him influence you in anything else. After all, how smart can he be if he's some sleazy detective?"

Quinn again cast a slow, sidelong glance at Cara, undisturbed by Peter Shelby. "I think I like *bogus* detective better than *sleazy.*"

"It does have a nicer ring to it," she agreed, glad Peter Shelby's petty name-calling couldn't get a rise out of him. "Are we finished here?"

"We need to take a look at your office, talk to anyone who might have been around the day of the wedding and check out the dressing room where you were last seen."

Cara nodded, then turned to Peter and Sheila. "I guess that's all, folks," she said.

Sheila's smile wasn't a smile at all, it was a pained grimace trying to be a smile. But at least she tried. Peter didn't even do that.

"Call the lawyer. Think about what I've said," he ordered. "The sooner we go through with the wedding the sooner we can get ourselves out of this mess."

Obviously the mess he was speaking of was not Cara's being shot or the total loss of her memory.

She merely inclined her head, purposely leaving him wondering whether or not she actually would contact the lawyer because she didn't like his dictatorial tone of voice. Then she and Quinn went to the door.

But just before leaving she couldn't resist turning one more time to face the dour duo. "Oh, and I'm just fine. Feeling great. No bad aftereffects of being shot—except that I can't remember anything. And yes, we're doing all we can to find out who did it. In the meantime, Quinn is making sure I'm safe. Thanks so much for asking. Your concern is touching."

Quinn gave them a thumbs-up. "Well done, guys," he said as he followed Cara out.

THE SEARCH of Cara's office and the dressing room she'd used to prepare for the wedding didn't offer any clues as to who shot her. No one they talked to at the hotel had seen or heard anything, either, though everyone seemed fond of Cara, as well as being genuinely anxious for her to return to work. In fact, some of them seemed almost desperate, letting it be known that she served as buffer between the employees and Peter and Sheila.

By then it was five-thirty. After making a stop in the rest-room, Cara rejoined Quinn just as he finished saying something to the desk clerk, and they went out to Quinn's car.

But once they got there, he didn't start the engine. He merely settled into the driver's seat, propped his left foot on the lower rim of the door and rested one elbow on the knee that poked up beside the steering wheel.

"Are we waiting for something?" Cara asked.

"The desk clerk says Peter and Sheila leave around six and they park in this lot. We're waiting to see what kind of car or cars they drive."

"Ooh, real P.I. work," she teased.

Quinn saluted her with one index finger poked momentarily to his temple and then pointed at her. "Bogus detective, at your service."

Cara laughed at him. "Serving idiotic amnesiacs."

"Servicing? Well, not all of them. Just one in particular."

The lot was along the south side of the hotel and they were parked near the rear of it, so most of the cars were in front of them, in plain view.

Cara repositioned herself, angling slightly toward Quinn so she could see both the front corner of the hotel and him.

She'd seen the way women had watched him as they worked their way through the Rosegate all afternoon, and it was no wonder to her. There was something so commanding about him, so forceful looking, so sexy...

Peter Shelby couldn't hold a candle to him.

Just sitting in the close confines of the car with him, breathing in the lingering scent of his after-shave, feeling his magnetism, made things inside of her flutter to life even without his teasing innuendos.

The memory of their night of lovemaking was fresh and just that flutter was enough to bring back vivid images of lying with him. Of his muscular arms encircling her. Of his legs twined with hers, his naked thigh up against her most private parts. Of his mouth covering hers, his tongue plundering. Of his hands all over her...

"Is it warm in here?" she wondered out loud, definitely feeling hot.

He rolled down the windows from a control panel on his door, but the air that came in didn't do much to cool the heat that was coming from inside of her. Especially not when she began to estimate how secluded their parking spot was and just how a man his size might be able to maneuver around the gear shift.

"So," she said then, forcing her thoughts back to business. "Do you think one of the errands Peter or Sheila ran yesterday was meant to be over me?"

"It's possible. It's also possible they were in this together the same as they seem to be in everything else."

"Mmm," Cara conceded, settling down a little more by staring at the building rather than at Quinn because her view of his profile caused her to think about how much he liked his earlobe nibbled. She swallowed back the urge to do some of that now. "But Tillie said they were only half an hour late to the wedding," she reminded. "That wouldn't have been time enough to shoot me, haul me into the mountains to dump me and then get back here."

"No, but it would have been time enough for them— or maybe just one of them—to shoot you, stash you somewhere so they could put in an appearance that would give them an alibi and then dispose of you later."

"Lovely," she said, wondering if the arousing thoughts of Quinn and the frustration of not having them fulfilled weren't better than picturing that scenario.

"What I'm wondering is, if the coincidence of the Shelbys knowing Nancy Sommers means anything," he said.

"And the fact that there seems to be something going on between her and Peter."

"Hard to miss that, wasn't it?"

Cara shivered and laughed at once. "Oh, I just had a disgusting thought. Nancy Sommers is about Sheila's same height, she has similar coloring and she has the same superior attitude. Do you think he has the hots for someone who reminds him of his mother?"

From the corner of her eye she saw Quinn's mouth stretch into that slow devil's smile. "What a sick mind you have," he said, as if the same thing had occurred to him.

"Blame it on my 'idiotic amnesia,'" she suggested. "I don't remind you of your mother, do I?"

"The secret's out," he joked, turning his head to look her in the eye. He clasped the back of her neck with one big hand to pull her toward him, meeting her nose to nose. "My mother is a meek, gray-haired woman twice your size, who would have never looked at what's happened to you as an adventure and an opportunity to play P.I. She'd have locked herself in her house and probably never come out again. No, you are nothing like my mother."

"So maybe I remind you of your father—that's even worse," she goaded.

Quinn rolled his eyes as if that were too outlandish to even answer. Instead he clasped the back of her neck and pulled her over to kiss her. His warm, moist lips parted over hers, and his tongue came to tease, acting out one part of her fantasy.

But just when she was really losing herself to that kiss, he stopped and sat back, dropping his hand to her knee for a squeeze that somehow promised more later. "We won't see them come out," he offered by way of explanation, sounding as reluctant not to pursue that kiss as she felt.

Just then Peter and Sheila Shelby came around the side of the hotel. Whatever they were discussing was serious because their heads were down slightly, they both wore dark frowns and they seemed to be talking very fast.

But they cut their conversation short when they reached the cars parked in the two slots nearest the front of the building, separating so that Peter could get into a white BMW that was several years old, and Sheila into an even older black Mercedes.

"Neither of those is the car that nearly ran us over, is it?" Cara asked.

"No. But that doesn't mean they didn't borrow or rent the one from yesterday."

"And what they said Nancy Sommers drives doesn't sound like it, either."

"Same answer."

They watched in silence as the mother and son swung out of their parking spots and then onto the street. Not until they were out of sight did Quinn start his car and do likewise.

"So here's what I'm thinking," Cara said with the flourish of her usual bigger-than-life imaginings. "Peter and Nancy Sommers are in passionate love and can't bear to be apart. Sheila thinks of Nancy as the daughter she never had and would like nothing better than to have Nancy marry her son. With me bumped off, Peter would inherit the whole trust and hotel right now, be free to marry Nancy, and they could all three live happily ever after.''

Only this time Quinn didn't roll his eyes or look at her as if she was crazy. He didn't even smile.

"You think I might be right this time?''

"I think it's a motive. And where you find a motive you're likely to find a perpetrator,'' he said quietly, lending more weight to the matter.

But Cara only felt a rush of excitement. "So how do we find out for sure and prove it?''

He sighed as if he didn't like what he was thinking. "We could take the long route—more investigating, checking alibis, asking questions.''

"*Or...*''

"Or I could set a trap, use Lindsey as a decoy and draw whoever it was out before they surprise us with another try at hurting you.''

Now *that* was what she'd imagined real P.I. work to be. A second rush of excitement skittered up her spine. "You don't need your sister to do it. I can be the decoy.''

"Not a chance,'' he decreed without skipping a beat.

She opened her mouth to protest but he cut her off before she got a word out.

"It's one thing to play at being a P.I. when we're doing legwork or asking questions in a reasonably controlled environment, Cara. But what I'm talking about now is deliberately baiting the likeliest suspects and setting up a trap into which one or more of them could be coming with the sole intent of doing you bodily harm. That's a whole different can of worms.''

"But you'd be right there, ready to spring the trap, wouldn't you?''

"It doesn't matter. Any number of things could go wrong. If they did—or even if they didn't—I can count on Lindsey to know what she's doing, to be able to handle herself, even to rescue me if the tables should turn somehow."

And he couldn't count on Cara for those things because she wasn't trained or experienced—that was the unspoken finish.

She knew he had a point, but it didn't change how much she wanted to be in on this.

"I mean it," he said then as if reading her mind, sounding tougher than she'd ever heard him before. "I wouldn't put any client at risk the way you're proposing, and I don't have personal feelings for other clients. I sure as hell wouldn't put you at risk. This is dangerous, and if I do it I will not have you in the middle of it."

"Lindsey doesn't look anything like me," she said, anyway.

"You're both the same size. If it was set up for after dark and the light bulb was taken out of the hallway fixture, the shadows would help. And with a wig and your clothes, and maybe that big floppy hat I seem to remember hanging on the side of the armoire, she'll pass."

"You could give me a gun to carry."

"I'm not kidding, Cara," he warned, and his tone made that eminently clear.

"But it wouldn't be right to endanger your sister on my account. Especially when I'm perfectly willing—"

"We don't need to discuss it anymore," he said as he pulled into the garage at his house.

"Using anyone but me could blow it completely," she went on arguing as though she hadn't heard him.

"If the culprit gets close enough to strike, he or she will also be close enough to see it isn't me and maybe not act at all. And without a second attempt we'll never be able to prove that whoever shows up didn't just stop by to say hi."

"We're gambling that whoever shows up won't expect a cup of coffee first," Quinn said facetiously. "That he or she will want to do the damage in a hurry and won't notice the disguise." He got out of the car and slammed the door hard for effect.

Cara got out, too, shutting her door normally. She met up with him at the garage entrance, seeing the dark frown that lined his heart-stoppingly handsome face. But she forged on in spite of it. "Even in a hurry they could notice. Beyond being the same height and weight, Lindsey and I don't look anything alike. But if I'm there they won't pull back at all and we'll have them cold!" She was really getting into the idea.

Quinn was not.

"Even if whoever shows up stops short of a murder attempt and makes up an excuse for being there, it will still give enough probable cause for suspicion for the police to get a warrant to search where they live, cars, offices, whatever seems likely to harbor evidence. It may not be as dramatic or as exciting, but that's too bad."

"I'm not afraid. I *want* to do this," she said firmly as he unlocked the back door.

"I don't care what you want. There's nothing in the world you could say that would change my mind. If I decide to do this I'll need you to set the trap—over the phone—and then that's it. I'll rent you an old Agatha Christie movie to keep you occupied while we're gone and that's as close to playing sleuth as you're going to get."

And his voice was loud enough to let her know he meant business.

Still, she tried once more "But—"

"No!" he shouted this time, a booming, daunting sound that said he was adamant.

Cara finally had to admit to herself that arguing it wasn't going to change his mind, so she didn't say any more.

But she thought, *We'll see...*

Chapter Ten

"I took out khaki pants and a white blouse—those seem to be the kind of thing I wear most—and a patchwork vest that I thought was distinctive enough to draw some attention," Cara said to Lindsey as they went into the bedroom at Quinn's house for Lindsey to get into her disguise the next evening. "But I still think it would be better for me to do this myself," she couldn't resist adding.

"I know this trap we've set up tonight seems like an adventure to you, a lark, but it's dangerous business. You have to take it seriously," Lindsey answered.

It definitely seemed like an adventure, but not a lark. "I'd take it very seriously," Cara assured. "I wouldn't do anything foolish."

"Your *going* would be foolish. We've baited three people—one or all of whom could have tried to kill you—so they'll try again. That isn't something you want to put yourself in line for."

"Better me than you. How could I live with myself if something happened to you that was aimed at me?"

"The point is, something is less likely to happen to me than to you because I know what I'm doing."

"I'd know what to do, too. It's a simple plan, after all. I'd go to the apartment and make plenty of noise letting myself in. Quinn snuck in three hours ago so Nancy Sommers wouldn't see him and he's probably already hiding. I'd just need to wait for someone to show up and signal him."

Lindsey shook her head, looking as stubborn as her brother. "Quinn doesn't want you there, Cara. His case, his call. I'm sorry."

"Yeah, me, too." Well, she'd given it the old college try. She forced herself to look disappointed but resigned, and teased, "But you're going to look silly in that wig."

Lindsey laughed. "Don't I know it. The hat will help, though."

Cara nodded toward the clothes she'd laid out on the bed. "I'll let you change so you can get this show on the road."

"It'll all be over before you know it," Lindsey assured in a voice that was so friendly and kind that it almost made Cara feel bad for what she was about to do.

Almost.

"I'll be downstairs, waiting for your grand entrance as me."

"See you in a few minutes."

Cara went downstairs all right. But she hardly sat calmly to wait for Quinn's sister.

Part of the plan involved using a spare key they'd found to bring Cara's car from the apartment. When it was driven back with Lindsey disguised as Cara at the wheel, it would appear to anyone who might be watching that she'd come alone, just as Cara had casually informed their suspects she would.

So she had only to take the key from the kitchen counter and slip out the back door.

Then came the tricky part.

She didn't know if Logan was home. His car wasn't in the drive the way Lindsey's was, but that didn't mean it wasn't in the garage. Or that a curious noise wouldn't bring him or Lindsey to investigate.

Keeping a wary eye on the carriage-house-apartment windows, she crossed the yard to Lindsey's tan station wagon and eased the driver's door open as carefully as any car thief.

Finding the lever that released the hood was easy but the pop that came with it sounded as loud as an alarm to her.

She shot glances up at Logan's place and then back at the house, but no one appeared.

Bolstered by that, Cara got out and went around to the front of the car to lift the hood.

If she'd ever known anything about automobile engines she didn't remember it and so really didn't have any idea how best to disable it. But there was no time to lose so she grabbed separate, important-looking wires in each hand and yanked, all the while hoping she wasn't doing anything really damaging.

Then, just for good measure, she unscrewed a wing nut that held a flying-saucer-shaped contraption in the center of it all and took the saucer-shaped contraption with her, content in the knowledge that Lindsey's car wasn't going anywhere anytime soon. And to make things even better, it was blocking the way if Logan's was in the garage.

With a last look at the house and apartment, she whispered, "Sorry, Lindsey," and hurried to her own jalopy parked on the street.

Starting it up was the next thing she thought might give her away, but once she had, she didn't wait around to find out. Instead she put it into gear, did a U-turn and hightailed it away from Quinn's house and siblings as fast as she could.

"Made it!" she breathed as she headed for the highway.

And that was when her thoughts turned to what, exactly, she was headed to.

The trap was simple. Cara had called Peter at home and informed him that she would only consider marrying him if he were to sign an ironclad agreement that he could do nothing to the Rosegate without her complete approval, and that were he to decide to comply, she would be alone at her apartment tonight where he could come to sign it.

The assumption had been that Peter would inform Sheila of this. But he'd been extremely upset and since the older woman was apparently nearby, she'd gotten on the extension to try talking Cara out of it. The end result was that they were both agitated and baited.

Then Cara had placed a call to Nancy Sommers. Once more she'd reached only an answering machine. After a futile attempt to get Nancy to pick up if she was there, Cara ended the call without leaving a message and dialed the manager to ask if he knew when Nancy was usually in.

He'd informed her that Nancy was there now, that he'd just seen her get home and her car was still in the lot.

Cara called again, this time knowing Nancy was listening, and left a message telling her neighbor when she'd be alone at the apartment and asking that Nancy come over to answer some questions for her.

And that was that. The trap was set. Cara had only to get to the apartment and wait for one or more of them to show up, at which point Quinn would step out of hiding and nab them.

She wasn't afraid. Excited, yes. On edge. But not frightened. Maybe what she was doing was foolish, but she had complete confidence in Quinn. And in her own ability to handle things.

What was more inclined to make her stomach lurch was the thought of Quinn.

He was not going to be happy to see her. Not by a long shot.

In fact, when she pulled into a parking spot at the apartment and turned off the engine, that knowledge caused her to pause for a moment. He was probably going to be downright mad.

"So what'll it be? You could go back, you know," she told herself.

But of course she wasn't going to do that. She'd come this far. She was certainly not flushing the whole plan now because she wasn't anxious to incur Quinn's wrath.

And she was courting danger to be sitting in the car thinking about it. It wasn't wise to give anyone the chance to strike in the parking lot.

"So, here goes."

She took a deep breath and got out of the car, making her way to the building while trying not to look around as if she were watching for someone. By the time she went through the security door her heart was racing. She climbed the stairs to the third floor, and once she was there she couldn't help keeping her eyes trained on Nancy Sommers's door.

What if the other woman was watching for her? What if she threw the door open and shot her right there in the hallway, before Quinn even knew she was out there?

Or what if Nancy and Peter and maybe even Sheila, too, were all in there, just waiting to drag her into the other apartment?

Cara's imagination was running at full speed and it made her hand shake as she unlocked her own apartment door. She pushed it halfway open and took one step inside when a bigger, stronger and decidedly steadier hand snaked out from behind it to yank her completely inside just before shutting the door firmly behind her.

"God, you scared me to death!" she whispered when she realized it was Quinn who had speeded her entrance.

"What the hell are you doing here?" he demanded, his voice no less fierce for the barely audible tone.

She shrugged. "I came to be the decoy."

"Where's Lindsey?"

"Stuck at home with car trouble I caused," she admitted reluctantly.

"Damn you!" he said through clenched teeth, shaking her one good shake before letting go of her wrist.

A sound in the hall silenced them both. Quinn put one eye to the peephole in the door then came away to say it was nobody that mattered.

"Shouldn't you hide before someone who does matter shows up?" Cara whispered in return.

He leaned down, his mouth so close to her ear she could feel the heat of his breath. "I'm going to take this up with you later," he threatened before slipping into the coat closet at the opposite end of the breakfast bar.

Cara took another deep breath and looked around at the disheveled state of a half-packed apartment, deciding she might as well make the most of the time.

Music seemed like a good idea, she thought. It would let it be known that she was there. She turned on the boom box, keeping the volume low so Quinn would still be able to hear anything that went on in the apartment. Then she crossed to the armoire and opened the doors.

She caught sight of herself in the mirrors on the inside of the doors and thought one look at her would give away that something was going on. Her cheeks were a bright, invigorated pink and she'd chewed off her lip gloss. She'd never make it as an undercover operative, she decided as she bent over to escape the odd sensation that came with her every glance in a mirror to put shoes from the bottom of the armoire into an empty packing box nearby.

Who would it be who took the bait of this trap? she wondered, imagining Sheila Shelby masterminding a plot to get rid of her, and Peter putting it into action like the angry puppet he seemed to be.

It had to be them. She really felt sure of it. They wanted the money, the hotel, the control. Certainly Peter wanted the freedom. And together they could offer each other moral support, not to mention alibis. Plus it made sense that moving Cara from the hotel dressing room and cleaning the blood in a hurry was more easily accomplished with the two of them working together and that would certainly account for their being late to the wedding. Top all of that off with that initial sense of foreboding she'd felt in facing Peter's office door, and Cara was absolutely convinced they were the culprits.

But would both of them show up here tonight? Or just Peter? Maybe Sheila would come, too, and wait in the car to act as lookout. Of course she would come. She'd have to be on hand to make sure Petey did the job right this time. And to be certain he didn't leave any incriminating evidence. And probably to help dispose of the body. Where did they plan to dump her this time? Someplace she was less likely to be discovered, was Cara's guess.

Finished with the shoes, she straightened just then.

But this time when she glanced at herself in the mirror she wasn't alone.

Her breath caught and lights flashed behind her eyes as images assaulted her, mixed and mingled, past and present.

She was in the dressing room at the hotel. Wearing the garish wedding gown, pushing at flounces and ruffles to get them to stay down. And then she'd looked up, into the mirror, into the reflection of the barrel of a gun pointed at her from behind.

Held by Nancy Sommers.

Then as now.

Cara hadn't heard her come in. Not into the dressing room. Not into the apartment. That and Cara's disorientation had cost critical seconds. Nancy Sommers was standing very close behind her. Too close.

Leaning slightly back into the armoire, Cara turned around to face her.

''Nancy!'' she finally managed, in genuine alarm and to alert Quinn. ''How'd you get in here?''

The statuesque woman held up the key ring Cara carried in her purse, the purse that the person who'd shot her would have, she thought with a flash of both recollection and deduction.

"Nancy," she said again in disbelief, a little louder, wondering why Quinn hadn't burst from the closet the first time. Then it occurred to her that maybe he was waiting to hear a confession and that she should get the other woman talking. "I didn't think it was you. I thought it must be Peter or Sheila who shot me."

"I can't believe you're not dead," she said disgustedly. "There was so much blood I was sure you were."

Did Quinn need to hear more than that? "But why?" she asked as that door to her memory eased its way open by slow inches. "We weren't enemies."

"I don't dislike you," the other woman answered matter-of-factly. "But I love Peter. And he loves me. We belong together. Not in two years or in twenty. Now. I wasn't going to stand by while he married you, watching from the sidelines, hoping we could be together someday, worrying that he might come to care about you the way your fathers wanted, left as nothing but the family friend." She spat the last words.

"So you decided to *shoot* me?" Cara asked in astonishment, her voice louder than it had been before.

"I decided to solve all of our problems. You can thank your father and Peter's for it. It's their fault for locking him up in that stupid will."

That seemed like confession enough. So where was Quinn?

Nancy inched the gun nearer to Cara's face. Her hand tightened around it and Cara's pulse went into triple time. She took a step sideways, toward the closet that secluded Quinn, and raised her voice an octave more as something else he might want to know occurred to her. "What about Peter? And Sheila? Are they in on this?"

"Of course not," she sneered. "As much as they'd like you out of the picture, they wouldn't do anything about it. They're neither one bold enough. I could see that it was up to me."

"It must not have been easy to do all you did with a roomful of wedding guests down the hall," Cara prompted, silently shrieking, *enough is enough, come out already!*

"It was easier than you think. I took a maid's uniform and a laundry cart from supply when no one was looking. Handy items, those laundry carts. I put you in it, mopped up the blood and then wheeled you through the delivery door."

She sounded proud of her accomplishment and it brought home just how dangerously disturbed this woman was. And how precarious was Cara's own position. Where the hell was Quinn? Surely he hadn't fallen asleep in the short time since he'd gone into that closet.

Cara swallowed, her mouth suddenly very dry. She tried to nonchalantly ease closer to the closet but this time Nancy Sommers didn't ignore it the way she had before.

"Stand still!"

Cara froze. But boy, what she wouldn't have given for one of the Strummels to appear from somewhere and come to her rescue! "Then what did you do with me?" she asked as if she weren't scared witless.

"I put you in the trunk of my car and left. I'd already told Peter I couldn't bear to come to that wedding, so no one was expecting me. I'd arranged to be out of town—that was my alibi. So I drove into the mountains to dump you in that field, and then back-tracked to Colorado Springs, where I spent the weekend thinking about my own wedding to Peter.''

Of course. After all, why let a little thing like murder mar your weekend? The woman really was nutso. "You must have been surprised to come back and find me here," Cara said.

"You'll never know. But then when your detective friend blabbed about the amnesia right away, I couldn't believe my luck. You didn't remember! That was almost too good to be true. I realized I'd been given a second chance."

"Which you used that day in the Springfield parking lot," Cara concluded. "It was you who tried to run me over."

"I went to the address on that business card, but that house is like a fortress, and with that cop living in back, I knew I couldn't do anything to you there. But I also knew you'd get around to that grandmother of yours sooner or later so I started to watch her. When you finally did I thought you'd stay with her. I figured it would be easy to get you there," she said with a full measure of the confidence she'd felt.

Then she smiled enormously at what she was about to say. "My car was having some repair work done and I had a rental the day you finally showed up. When you came out, I thought, *Why wait? Why not do it now, with the car?* It didn't belong to me, anyway, and the windows were tinted so nobody could see me. Hit-and-run accidents happen and you rarely hear about them being solved. And it occurred to me that if after I hit you I ran the car into something, that accident would camouflage any damage from you. It seemed like the perfect plan. But I swear, you're like a cat. You must have nine lives."

Cara certainly hoped so. "Well, here's what I'm thinking," she said as if confiding in her best friend. She glanced around hoping it looked as if her eyes were just wandering when in fact she was searching for a means of escape or a weapon of her own. "How about if I just don't marry Peter? That certainly seems like a better solution than this. Nothing says we *have* to comply with the will. We can just wait it out."

Nancy's expression turned ugly. "Don't take me for a fool!" she shouted. "You're not going to do that. You need that trust money and the hotel worse than Peter and Sheila do. You said yourself that you had to get hold of it, no matter what it took, even if it meant spending the next twenty years of your life in a phony marriage. You didn't have a choice."

Nancy seemed to be tiring of the conversation because she raised the gun from where it had drifted downward as she'd talked, to the middle of Cara's face once more.

"You don't want to do this, Nancy," she said in a hurry, retreating in spite of her confident tone.

Nancy followed, step for step. "Oh, but I do," she assured.

Everything suddenly seemed to move in slow motion. Cara saw the other woman take her final aim, her finger tighten against the trigger—

"Quinn!" she screamed as she lunged for the nearest lamp, swinging it at her assailant. She hit Nancy's gun hand at the same moment a shot fired and the closet door splintered as Quinn burst through it to hit Nancy with a full body tackle that knocked them both to the floor.

But Nancy was not a small woman and she clearly had no intention of giving up easily. Kicking and clawing, she fought as fiercely as a man.

Quinn had her wrist in the grip of one hand, keeping the gun raised above their bodies as Nancy struggled to lower it, to use it against him.

Cara picked up another lamp, intent on bashing Nancy if only she could do it without hurting Quinn.

Then one more shot rang out and Quinn finally overpowered her, wresting the gun out of her grip and pinning her facedown on the carpet just as Logan and Lindsey rushed through the apartment door.

Adrenaline was pumping through Cara even as a delayed reaction to fear kicked the starch out of her knees. She closed her eyes and sank to the arm of the sofa to catch her breath and wait for her pulse to stop pounding in her ears.

Then Quinn was beside her, pulling her into the crushing circle of his arms as if he needed the reassurance as much as she did.

"Are you all right?" he asked in a gruff voice.

Being against him renewed her sense of security. Logan was handcuffing Nancy Sommers. Lindsey was calling the local police. And as frightening as the whole thing had been, it had also been exhilarating.

Cara looked up at Quinn's handsome face. His expression showed concern, a stern frustration and the anger he'd gone into the closet with in the first place. But Cara could only grin at him.

"I'm okay. But I just remembered—sometimes that closet door sticks."

"THAT'S RIGHT, my memory is as good as new. The amnesia is completely gone," Cara assured her grandmother later that night when she and Quinn finally got back to his house.

Talking to Tillie—*remembering* Tillie—felt good. Great. Like coming home. Cara adored the old woman who had been a kindred spirit and her best friend throughout her life. Now that that relationship, as well as everything else, was all within her mental grasp again it was hard to believe that anything had been able to take it away. But Cara was grateful to have it returned.

"Are you still at your apartment?" Tillie asked.

"No, I'm staying at Quinn's place. For one more night, anyway," she said, those last words quieter than the others.

"And then what?"

And then it was back to real life. "Oh, I don't know, Gram. Ask me that when I come by in the morning," she said because remembering it all didn't mean she wanted to think about it. Not tonight. The slate wasn't clean anymore and she had to deal with that. But not before having just one more night with Quinn.

"You're sure you're all right?" her grandmother repeated yet again.

"Yep. Just fine. Go on to bed and get some sleep."

Tillie finally agreed to let her off the phone. They said their good-nights and Cara hung up.

She was alone in the kitchen and she'd been facing the cupboards as she talked to her grandmother. Now she turned to lean into the counter, taking a deep breath and sighing it out.

It had been a long evening. The local police had come to arrest Nancy Sommers and ask their endless questions to compile their reports. And into the commotion Peter and Sheila Shelby had come, intent on talking Cara out of the notion of an agreement that gave her the power to veto what they wanted to do with the Rosegate. It hadn't helped matters that they'd found the woman they both cared about in handcuffs, accused of two counts of attempted murder. What a mess.

But it was all over now and Cara didn't want to think about it any more than she wanted to think about her past. Or what she was going to do with her future.

Putting everything out of her mind was easier when Quinn came into the room.

He was still mad at her. He hadn't said a half dozen words to her since making sure she was okay and he didn't add to that count now.

He went to the wine rack and chose a bottle from among the six that were there, uncorking it. Then he took two glasses from the cupboard, and with those in one hand and the wine in the other he came to stand so close in front of her he was almost on top of her. And if that wasn't enough, he leaned forward, forcing her nearly into a back bend, his nose a scant inch from hers.

"There's a part of me that would like to turn you over my knee for that stunt you pulled tonight," he said with full evidence of how angry it had made him.

"It all worked out for the best, though," she reminded him. "The police got to the apartment quick because of Logan calling them when he realized he and Lindsey were stuck here. Lindsey's car is back together and working just fine—again, thanks to Logan and his skills as a mechanic. Lindsey doesn't have any hard feelings about my outmaneuvering her. And she couldn't have done anything much differently with Nancy than I did. In fact, she might not have gotten as full a confession because once Nancy realized it wasn't me, she might have just run."

He leaned even closer, his brows pulled over steely eyes. "You don't want to argue this with me."

She believed him. "Okay, so if only part of you wants to turn me over your knee, what does the other part want to do?" she prompted hopefully.

"It has another position in mind." He straightened and pointed a single index finger toward the ceiling. "There's a full bathtub waiting. If you're interested."

Cara smiled at him. "I'm interested."

"Go on up. I'll lock the doors and be there in a minute."

That was a command she was more than willing to obey.

She knew the tub was a fancy one, with whirlpool jets. But she'd never taken the time to explore the mysterious purposes of all the dials and knobs. Now she found it a gently swirling caldron of opalescent bubbles glimmering with the reflected glow of candles set all over the otherwise dark bathroom.

"If I'd have known this was the consequence of making him mad, I'd have done it before," she said to herself as she shed her clothes and sank into the water that buoyed bubbles to her chin.

And if that wasn't blissful enough, she even got to watch as Quinn stripped down when he joined her a few minutes later, the golden light gilding his magnificent body.

Not until he'd slipped into the opposite end of the tub, a long leg on either side of her, did he reach for the wine and glasses he'd set on the nearby vanity top. After pouring them each a liberal amount and handing

Cara hers, he settled back and took a sip. Then he pinned her with eyes that still bore traces of anger.

"I'd say that in a similar situation, don't ever ignore what I tell you again, but I hope there'll never be a similar situation."

Cara ran a toe up the inside of his thigh, stopping just short of anything important. "Are you telling me my adventures are over?"

"Any dangerous ones are. At least they'd better be. And are you really okay?"

"One hundred percent. Want to grill me about my past to prove it?"

He rested his head against the wall behind him. "Why don't you just tell me about yourself."

"I can do that." She settled back the same way he was and sipped her wine. "I graduated from Arvada West High School and went to the University of Colorado at Denver because it was within walking distance of the Rosegate, which meant I could work there at the same time. I'll be thirty-one in four months, on the thirteenth of January. I'm the only child of Mona and Eddie Walsh. My folks were killed in a car accident when a drunk driver ran a red light. It was Leo Shelby's birthday, and even though neither of my parents were fond of Sheila, they were close to Leo. The two couples were supposed to go out to celebrate. At the last minute Sheila didn't go and it saved her life."

"And threw yours into a tizzy," Quinn offered.

"You know that part."

"Tell me about Tillie."

"She's terrific. Fun and funny and she's always loved me absolutely unconditionally. Remember the house in my dream, the one near the highway that we went to?"

He nodded over his glass.

"Tillie lived there before her arthritis got the better of her and I spent almost every weekend with her all through my growing-up years. That was why the house was familiar."

He gave a breathy little laugh, the first evidence she'd seen that he was easing out of his anger. "Strange. So you spent a lot of time only a few blocks from me and we never ran into each other. Yet years later we meet up under the most bizarre circumstances, miles away."

"Destiny?" she suggested.

He raised a conceding eyebrow and took another sip of his wine. Then he said, "Why can't Tillie be cared for at home?"

"A lot of reasons. At Springfield she has a sort of crane to help her into and out of bed, and the bathroom is outfitted for her needs, too. There are emergency buttons all over the place in case she needs help, which she does pretty often, as well as a sort of bed check morning, noon and night to make sure she's not in trouble and can't even reach one of those. There are trained people on staff to help her bathe, and physical therapists who work with her to prevent her from getting any more crippled than she has to. Those are all things she needs that I can't supply or do for her myself in a private setting. Plus—and this is a huge plus—she can have all of that along with her independence. That's very, very important to her."

"And to you, too," he added solemnly.

"And to me, too."

For a moment he seemed to mull that over. Then he ran his ankle up her side and said, "Tell me about your love life," in a voice grown suddenly smoky.

"This is it," she answered with a laugh that sounded sensual even though that hadn't been her intention.

"Nearly thirty-one and you've never been involved with anybody?"

"Not never, but it's been a while. There were a couple of guys whose company I enjoyed before the accident—in spite of my father's disapproval and attempt to put me together with Peter. But the hotel was my passion. Then, after the accident, when I had to take over doing everything for Tillie that my folks did on top of what I did normally, well—" she shrugged "—there just hasn't been a time or place for romance in my life."

"So you decided to go ahead and marry old Peter."

Cara didn't want to talk about that. The most she would say was "It wasn't a matter of nothing better to do."

Then she slid down just a little farther in the water, making contact between the arches of her feet and his most private parts. "Anything else you're dying to know?"

He stared into her eyes as a slow, sexy smile raised both corners of his mouth, one slightly ahead of the other. But he didn't say anything. Instead he threw back the rest of his wine and replaced the glass on the vanity. Then he took hold of her ankles and pulled her toward him, wrapping her legs around his waist as he slid to the center of the tub.

He cupped her rear end to position her just so atop his thighs, put her wineglass with his and then trailed his hands up her back as he captured her lips in an openmouthed kiss.

Cara followed his lead, willing, eager for what she now knew was unlike anything she'd ever experienced before, for this man was unlike anyone she'd ever known.

The bubbles tickled her already-erect nipples and she tightened her legs so that she came fully up against him.

He was definitely not mad at her anymore.

Or if he was, he was capable of being eloquently aroused at the same time.

Passion ignited between them instantly. Hungry, urgent passion that didn't care if water sloshed onto the floor, that didn't care about anything but being gloried in.

They made love in a wet, slippery, bubbly frenzy that was really only an appetizer, for when the water and their immediate needs were cooled, they moved to his big bed where they'd barely pulled back the covers before he took her again.

And then again and again throughout the night.

Each time grew slower than the one before as passion calmed enough to let them savor what was between them, what they could each do to the other, the love they shared, until coming together just before dawn had a final poignancy for Cara that was almost too sweet to bear.

The blanket and sheets were so disheveled by then they were like a cocoon around them, and lying there, their exhausted bodies melded together, Quinn whispered that he loved her.

"I love you, too," she answered in a voice choked with the well of emotions that suddenly rose inside of her.

"Are you okay?"

"Just tired," she lied.

But apparently she was convincing enough because he only sighed his agreement as his arms relaxed around her and he settled into sleep.

And then she closed her eyes, too, as much to block out the sight of the first glimmer of sunshine as to sleep.

For with the new day came the old life.

And she knew she would have to face it.

Alone.

Chapter Eleven

There had never been a case Quinn regretted solving.

Until now.

He was alone in bed when he woke up late the next morning. Sounds of Cara moving around in the room next to his drifted through the wall. She was getting dressed, he assumed. He rolled to his back, listening to her. Loving her.

But what was he going to do about it?

He knew what he wanted to do about it.

He wanted her in his life permanently. In his house. In his bed. He wanted her as his wife.

He sure as hell didn't want her to be Peter Shelby's wife.

But asking her to marry him instead was asking a lot.

He could give her many things, but he couldn't give her the well-padded trust fund or the twelve-story hotel she needed to support her grandmother. And so to ask her to marry him was to ask her to accept so much less.

Quinn took a deep breath, ran his hands through his hair and then blew the air out in a long, slow gust.

In his mind's eye he could see her as clearly as if she were in the room with him. Her long straight hair glistening with bourbon-colored streaks. That delicate body moving agilely, gracefully. Those violet eyes aglimmer with fun and humor as her imagination did leaps and bounds through God only knew what.

Just thinking about her made him smile. He loved her spirit, her outlook, her energy.

How could he stand to know that it would be stomped on by Peter and Sheila Shelby instead of reveled in by him?

He couldn't.

So what was he going to do about it?

Everything he considered seemed so damned selfish.

But wasn't what they had together too important not to be? Wasn't it more important than money or a pile of bricks and mortar?

It was to him. It was worth anything to him. It was worth everything to him.

And if that meant he had to be selfish, well, he'd make up for it later—somehow—but selfish was what he was going to be.

He just hoped to God that what they had together was more important to Cara, too.

CARA WAS PUTTING the last of her things in the same packing box she'd used to bring them from the apartment when Quinn appeared at her bedroom door.

It was criminal for a man to look that good right out of bed, with his hair sleep-tousled and his face whisker-shadowed. But one glance at him leaning a broad shoulder against the doorjamb, his arms crossed over his naked chest, wearing nothing but a pair of black-silk boxer shorts, was enough for Cara's heart to give a kick.

"Hi," she said, trying to sound bright when she felt anything but.

He pointed his chin at the box. "Good idea. I'll clear you a couple of drawers and some space in my closet so we can free this room."

Cara couldn't look at him and say what she had to, so she took a blouse off a hanger and began to fold it very meticulously. "You know that's not what I'm doing," she said quietly.

"What *are* you doing?

"Packing up all my cares and woes?" If she could joke through this it would be easier, she thought.

"To take them where?"

She shrugged. "Back."

"You don't have to."

Since awakening this morning she'd played a number of scenarios through her mind, all of them having to do with exclamations of love and promises of forever. But they were only fantasies. And today was a day for facing reality. "I have to become Mrs. Whos-its."

"You don't *have* to do anything."

"I do, though."

"Why?"

Again the shrug, more brittle than the one before. "I agreed to marry Peter in the first place because things had degenerated to the point where there just wasn't . . . isn't another option. I've exhausted all my credit and cut every corner there is to cut and I'm going under. Fast."

"Then let me be your life preserver."

It almost physically hurt her to have him say that. It was so tempting. It was what she'd fantasized. But she couldn't do it.

He went on before she could say anything. "Marry me, Cara."

"I can't," she whispered.

"You love me. You want to."

"I can't," she said more strongly.

"I'll support you. You'll support Tillie. It's as easy as that."

If only that were true. She set the folded blouse in the box as carefully as if it were ancient pottery and wrapped an arm around one of the bed's four posters. She shrugged again, but this time her shoulders seemed to stick before she could get them down. "I can't let you do that."

"Why not?"

"It isn't fair. It isn't right."

He chuckled what was really no more than a burst of mirthless air. "I'm asking you to give up what I assume is a lot of money and ownership of a hotel you love for me. What's fair or right about that?"

"Actually, I thought it was really nice of you."

"But you won't do it."

"I'd be your charity case—for good instead of just for these last days."

"You'd be my *wife*."

"A wife who came to you with a mountain of debt and tons more of expenses in the future for an old lady you don't even know." She shivered and made a face she hoped was comically pained. "What a terrible way to start a marriage—strapping you with all that."

"I don't give a damn about any of that. It's you I want."

"Oh sure, that's easy for you to say," she joked once more.

"Yes, it is."

"But the reality is a lot different. I know. I've lived it for the last three years. We're talking some big bills here, some major responsibility."

"So?" he asked, clearly not taking it as seriously as she was, as she knew he should.

"So I decided the most reasonable route was to go through with the phony marriage so the inheritance will solve the immediate money problems and pave the way to contest the will. If it gets thrown out, and if you still want me when it does—" her voice caught and she had to clear her throat to recover. "I'll be free."

"Two years from now. And if the will doesn't get thrown out you'll be tied to Shelby for a hell of a lot longer than that. It stinks."

"But it's the only chance of beating this mess."

"Half a chance isn't a good gamble. Not when we have so much at stake."

Looking at him was such agony she couldn't bear it any more, so she took the last shirt off its hanger, folding this one with agitated swipes. "I know it isn't pretty, but it's what I've decided to do."

"For money?" he demanded in disbelief.

"You make it sound like greed and that's not what it is. I don't want to come to you carrying along so many burdens. I'm afraid it would eat away at you and me both, at our relationship, at our marriage."

"I was thinking more along the lines of sharing your burdens the same way I'll expect you to share mine. All we'd be doing is pooling our resources and taking care of what needs to be taken care of out of that."

"Except that you'd be coming in with all the assets and I'd be coming in with all the debts. You'd be getting a raw deal, Strummel."

"So keep a tab, if it makes you happy," he said impatiently. "When you get your inheritance you can settle up. I don't mind waiting twenty years. Or I'll front you the money to contest the will. But don't walk out of here."

Putting the second shirt into the box finished her packing. For a moment she stared into her belongings, knowing that there was nothing left to keep her there. No pretense, anyway. Quinn and her feelings for him were certainly enough, but Quinn and her feelings for him were the reason she'd decided she had to go through with this.

She picked up the box and with a very straight back went to face him at the door. "Give me two years so we can have a chance of being together without all the baggage. We deserve a clean slate, Quinn. We deserve for things to be as good as they have been."

"Two years," he repeated. "And what do we do during that time? Have lunch occasionally?" He shook his head and stretched one arm across the doorway even though his body was a barricade all on its own. "I'm not going to let you go."

"Don't force me to lock you in the closet," she deadpanned, still trying desperately to make light of what was not.

He didn't say anything to that, and she was left looking into those silver eyes.

Somewhere in the back of her mind a little voice asked her what she was doing.

But she ignored it.

"Tell me you don't love me," Quinn demanded. "Tell me you don't want to marry me. Because those are the only two reasons I'll accept."

"Don't make this any harder than it is."

"It kills me to see that it isn't so hard you can't do it."

The raw pain that echoed in his voice cut her like broken glass. She'd only been trying to make this easier somehow, but clearly she'd failed.

"I have to. I have to get out from under the problems I'm in before we can be together. Marriage is tough enough, risky enough these days without going into it with built-in pitfalls. I only want to do it with a clean slate," she repeated forcefully. "We deserve that."

"Nobody comes with a clean slate," he answered in a voice low and controlled.

"Okay, so what's on yours? What problems would you be bringing to match mine?"

He only countered with another question. "Would you not want me if our circumstances were reversed?"

"But they aren't."

He raised an eyebrow at her as if he was still waiting for an answer. But it was the best she could do.

"Thanks for everything," she said in a barely audible voice, hating how inane it sounded.

"Put the box down and let's go back to bed."

She shook her head, standing her ground.

"I won't play 'let's do lunch' for two years," he warned her. "Or twenty. If you walk out of here it's over. You might as well stay married to Shelby for the rest of your life."

Quinn was angry again and the thoughts she'd had the night before about the wonderful consequences of making him mad flashed through her mind. But she knew the consequences this time wouldn't be so wonderful.

Still, she had to hope they wouldn't be as bad as he threatened. That when he cooled off he'd see she was only thinking of him, of the health of their relationship. And he'd wait for her.

"I have to go," she said around a horrible tightness in her chest.

He stared into her eyes as if he could change her mind through the pure force of his will. But she didn't waver. "I've made my decision," she added for good measure, sounding strong even though she felt weak enough to wilt.

Anger seemed to yank him off the jamb then and swing him into the hall, freeing the way and silently challenging her, she knew, to actually go.

She stepped through the door with every intention of doing just that. But for some reason she stalled, meeting his furious gaze.

She reminded herself that this was best for everyone. And yet it didn't keep instant tears from flooding her eyes. Before he could see them, she turned away and headed for the stairs.

What are you doing? that little voice in the back of her mind shrieked, louder this time, stopping her on the edge of that first step.

She was doing what she thought was right.

So why did it feel so bad?

Looking down those stairs at the front door was like staring into a black hole. Being shot, left for dead, losing her memory, hadn't been as weighty as the thought of descending those stairs and walking out that door.

Of course she'd had Quinn's help through everything else.

Now she was going back to what she'd borne alone for a long time, and somehow even the thought of finally having enough money and inheriting the hotel didn't make leaving seem any easier.

Only the idea of having Quinn by her side made anything seem worthwhile.

The temptation was enormous.

She shook her head to get rid of it and ordered herself to go down those stairs.

The problems and responsibilities that she faced were her own. She'd get them under control, taken care of, and then she and Quinn could be together. It was the reasonable, rational route.

Practical but painful.

His last words reverberated through her mind with a will of their own.

Would she not want him if their circumstances were reversed?

Silly question.

It wouldn't change how she felt about him. It wouldn't make her love him any less.

But still...

It was much easier, she realized, to be the giver than the receiver. She could provide for Tillie gladly, which she'd done in spite of the difficulties. But to accept the same kind of help from Quinn? That was harder.

Then something else occurred to her. In all of the difficulties that had come out of providing for Tillie, nothing had changed her feelings for her grandmother. She loved the old woman just the same. In fact, she was willing to do anything—even marry Peter Shelby—to be able to go on doing for Tillie. So wasn't it possible that if Quinn truly loved her, helping her wouldn't be the burden she thought?

And she did believe that Quinn truly loved her.

As much as she loved him.

So what are you doing? that little voice asked yet again as those stairs stretched out before her.

She didn't know how long she'd been standing there, but he hadn't said a word the entire time. He was waiting, she knew, for her to choose to stay. For her to choose him.

But could she? Should she?

"I don't love my grandmother any less because she needs my help," she heard herself say ruminatively, without turning more than her head to her shoulder.

"Good point," he said in a low, dark voice.

"And you're right, if our positions were reversed, this would not be such a big deal to me."

"It shouldn't be a big deal to you now."

She pivoted enough to lean against the wall much the same way he was. "But it is."

He looked over at her, his expression solemn. Then he came off the wall to stand very near, placing both hands on either side of her head to do a partial push-up over the box she still held as the monument to her indecision. "Do you love me, Cara?" he asked in a strong, quiet, calming tone that seemed intent on leading her through these murky waters.

"You know I do."

"Do you want to marry me?"

"You know the answer to that, too. Yes, I want to marry you."

"Then listen carefully to this, because I mean it *Nothing else matters*. It's all just details we can handle. Together, just like any other married couple."

Lord, but she wanted to believe that. She looked up into that face she adored, those eyes that could melt her heart with only a glance, and she honestly didn't know how she could possibly walk away from him. From her feelings for him.

So believe him, that little voice advised.

She wanted to.

And she really didn't have a choice.

She had to trust that the flotsam she brought with her was only incidental to what they felt for one another.

Because otherwise she wouldn't have him at all.

She took a deep breath and exhaled her doubts along with the air. Then, as if there hadn't been any mental agonizing at all, she said, "So I was thinking that maybe old Peter Whos-its and I could try to get Sheila out on the payroll as his assistant. It would give them two incomes. It wouldn't be enough for them to keep their staff, or put them back on the society pages, but they'd be able to survive."

"They'd do fine."

"And if I borrowed the money from you to contest the will, it would only be a loan, repayable with interest."

One side of his mouth floated upward as he countered with a lascivious demand. "And I get to say how that interest is paid."

"Deal." She raised a hand to his cheek, loving him, knowing she'd been out of her mind to think that she could live for two years without him when she hadn't been able to last even two minutes. But still she felt obliged to say, "Are you sure you wouldn't like to look over my bills before—"

He stopped her words with his mouth over hers in kiss that claimed her. Then he said, "There are othe things I'd rather look over."

"You mean you didn't see enough last night?"

"I'll never get enough."

"That's good because you may have to hang aroun for twenty years to recoup your investment."

"I think I can handle that."

She couldn't resist a grin. "And in the meantime you can always use my talents as a P.I. when the nee arises."

He rolled his eyes at that, shook his head and the kissed her again, a long, slow kiss that said they had a the time in the world. "You stick to running your ho tel and I'll try to handle being a P.I. on my own," b answered when it was over.

"It won't be nearly as much fun," she warned.

"No doubt. You'll just have to make it up to m when we get to bed at night."

"I can do that."

"Prove it."

She wiggled her eyebrows at him and arched up wit an openmouthed kiss of her own. Then she ducked ou from under him to set the packing box down, grabbe hold of the waistband of his shorts and led him to hi room, where she closed the door firmly behind them shutting out the rest of the world.

"I really do love you," she said as a rush of pur gratitude went through her for the destiny that ha brought them together.

His smile was devilish and sexy. "Prove it," he re peated.

"Only on one condition."

"What's that?"

"That you be the one to answer to Peter Whos-its for borrowing his bride. He's not going to be happy about this, you know."

"I can do that," Quinn assured. "Only I'm not borrowing you. You're mine for good."

"Yes, I am," she said as she slipped into his arms.

Chapter Twelve

Lindsey was happy that things had worked out for he
brother and Cara as she drove to Quinn's house th
next day for the champagne brunch to celebrate. An
the fact that they were getting married, that Quin
would be busy with wedding plans and setting u
housekeeping, put the seal on Lindsey's own decisio
to get back to work.

With the exception of a few background checks an
agreeing to pose as Cara—whose ruse she still couldn'
believe she'd fallen for—Lindsey hadn't taken a cas
since her divorce.

Quinn had been patient with her. More patient tha
she'd been with herself. As the only girl with two olde
brothers she'd grown up a tough-as-nails tombo
who'd sooner have died than show weakness or vul
nerability. She guessed that early practice at buryin
her emotions had made her think she didn't have man
or that she could control what she did have.

Well, she'd learned differently. It had shocked her t
find herself so devastated by her divorce that she hadn'
been able to concentrate.

Of course it didn't help that the divorce had lande
a double blow with the loss of Bobby. That was ever

bit as hard to handle as the disastrous end of her marriage. Maybe harder.

But there was a time to grieve and brood and feel rotten, and she'd done plenty of that. Enough to get her house in order again, the actual physical gaps in furniture and belongings filled. But enough was enough and now the time had come to pick herself up by the bootstraps and go on.

Actually she was looking forward to working again, she thought as she pulled into Quinn's driveway. Even the thought of getting involved at the end of Cara's case had gotten her juices flowing. An adult environment, away from any reminders of kids or motherhood was very appealing. And certainly P.I. work offered that.

She went in the back door and found Quinn and Logan at the kitchen table.

"There's plenty to do here," Quinn was assuring Logan. "Don't forget you have the option of a full partnership with Lindsey and me if you quit."

Lindsey didn't have to ask to know they were talking about Logan's problems on the police force again. "That's true," she confirmed, joining the discussion without skipping a beat. "We'd be glad to have you."

"You could keep Strummel Investigations from closing up shop while I'm on my honeymoon," Quinn added, as if it were incentive.

"Well, actually," Lindsey put in, "we won't need to shut down then. I'll be here."

Both of her brothers' gazes suddenly trained on her.

"I'm coming back. Full-time," she announced to their questioning stares.

For a moment neither of them said anything. They just watched her as if waiting for the punch line. Then

Quinn's skepticism found voice. "Are you sure you're ready for that?"

"I'm sure," she said forcefully, to dispel his doubts.

From the look on his face, it didn't. "Maybe you should just ease back in," he suggested. "Serve a few summons, do more background checks, maybe a surveillance or two."

She appreciated his concern, but she wouldn't accept it. "Sorry, I'm through doing all the detail work while you get to do the interesting stuff," she teased. Then she went on more seriously. "This is what I need now—to get out of my house and be busy again. And don't say anything about Cara getting away from me," she warned when she saw it coming. "You weren't exactly on guard with her, either, or we wouldn't be here at your engagement party, would we?"

"She's got you there," Logan said as if awarding points. "Besides, I think it'd be good for her to get back to work."

Still Quinn looked dubious. But after a while he sighed and conceded. "I'm not your keeper. If you say you're ready to come back, then come back. In fact I just took a message off the answering machine for something you can handle, if you want it."

"Great." This was the right decision, Lindsey realized when her spirits and energy level took a sudden leap at the thought of a new case. "Fill me in."

But just then the sound of Cara pulling into the driveway drew Quinn's attention. "I took down the information and left it on my desk. Look it over while I help Cara get her grandmother inside," he suggested.

Quinn and Logan both headed out the back door while Lindsey went to the office she and her brother shared. She felt rejuvenated as she searched for and found the legal pad on which he'd noted the message.

But it was short-lived.

"So much for being in an adult environment, away from anything to do with kids or motherhood," Lindsey muttered to herself when she read the note, thinking that fate had a strong sense of irony and wavering in her decision to take this on.

Quinn would do it if she didn't want to, she knew. But the idea of that, of admitting to him that she still might have some raw wounds, was unappealing.

Besides, she had to get back into the flow of things and the world was full of kids and babies and other reminders of what hadn't worked out in her own life.

"Now or never," she murmured, as if sounding a battle cry as she reread the note.

Someone named Graham Dunn had called to hire Strummel Investigations. It seemed he'd come home from an early-morning jog to find twin babies sitting in the middle of his bedroom floor. He'd never seen them before, had no idea who they were, who they belonged to, where they'd come from, how they got there or why they'd been left with him.

And he needed to hire someone to figure it all out....

Once in a while, there's a story so special, a story so unusual,
that your pulse races, your blood rushes. We call this

HART'S DREAM is one such story.

At first they were dreams—strangely erotic. Then visions—strikingly real. Ever since his accident, when Dr. Sara Carr's sweet voice was his only lifeline, Daniel Hart couldn't get the woman off his mind. Months later it was more than a figment of his imagination calling to him, luring him, doing things to him that only a flesh-and-blood woman could.... But Sara was nowhere to be found....

#589 HART'S DREAM
by
Mary Anne Wilson

Available in July wherever Harlequin books are sold. Watch for more Heartbeat
stories, coming your way—only from American Romance!

HEART9

A NEW STAR COMES OUT TO SHINE....

American Romance continues to search the heavens for the best new talent... the best new stories.

Join us next month when a new star appears in the American Romance constellation:

**Charlotte Douglas
#591 IT'S ABOUT TIME
July 1995**

When Tory Caswell attended her sister's wedding in a magical old Victorian resort, her mind was filled with images of bouquets and garters. But when she awakened the next morning, she thought she was still dreaming. A gray-eyed hunk was next to her in bed! And he claimed he'd come from the 1800s....

RISING STAR

Be sure to Catch a "Rising Star"!

ANNOUNCING THE

PRIZE SURPRISE SWEEPSTAKES!

This month's prize:

L-A-R-G-E—SCREEN PANASONIC TV!

This month, as a special surprise, we're giving away a fabulous FREE TV!

Imagine how delighted you and your family will be to own this brand-new 31" Panasonic** television! It comes with all the latest high-tech features, like a SuperFlat picture tube for a clear, crisp picture...unified remote control...closed-caption decoder...clock and sleep timer, and much more!

The facing page contains two Entry Coupons (as does every book you received this shipment). Complete and return *all* the entry coupons; **the more times you enter, the better your chances of winning the TV!**

Then keep your fingers crossed, because you'll find out by July 15, 1995 if you're the winner!

Remember: The more times you enter, the better your chances of winning!*

PTV KAL

PRIZE SURPRISE
SWEEPSTAKES
OFFICIAL ENTRY COUPON

This entry must be received by: JUNE 30, 1995
This month's winner will be notified by: JULY 15, 1995

YES, I want to win the Panasonic 31" TV! Please enter me in the drawing and let me know if I've won!

Name_____

Address _____Apt. _____

City   State/Prov.   Zip/Postal Code

Account #_____

Return entry with invoice in reply envelope.

© 1995 HARLEQUIN ENTERPRISES LTD.   CTV KAL

PRIZE SURPRISE
SWEEPSTAKES
OFFICIAL ENTRY COUPON

This entry must be received by: JUNE 30, 1995
This month's winner will be notified by: JULY 15, 1995

YES, I want to win the Panasonic 31" TV! Please enter me in the drawing and let me know if I've won!

Name_____

Address _____Apt. _____

City   State/Prov.   Zip/Postal Code

Account #_____

Return entry with invoice in reply envelope.

© 1995 HARLEQUIN ENTERPRISES LTD.   CTV KAL

OFFICIAL RULES

PRIZE SURPRISE SWEEPSTAKES 3448

NO PURCHASE OR OBLIGATION NECESSARY

Three Harlequin Reader Service 1995 shipments will contain respectively, coupon for entry into three different prize drawings, one for a Panasonic 31" wide-screen TV another for a 5-piece Wedgwood china service for eight and the third for a Sharp ViewCam camcorder. To enter any drawing using an Entry Coupon, simply complete and mail according to directions.

There is no obligation to continue using the Reader Service to enter and be eligible for any prize drawing. You may also enter any drawing by hand printing the words "Prize Surprise," your name and address on a 3"x5" card and the name of the prize you wish that entry to be considered for (i.e., Panasonic wide-screen TV, Wedgwood china or Sharp ViewCam). Send your 3"x5" entries via first-class mail (limit: one per envelope) to: Prize Surprise Sweepstakes 3448, c/o the prize you wish that entry to be considered for, P.O. Box 1315, Buffalo, NY 14269-1315, USA or P.O. Box 610 Fort Erie, Ontario L2A 5X3, Canada.

To be eligible for the Panasonic wide-screen TV, entries must be received by 6/30/95; for the Wedgwood china, 8/30/95; and for the Sharp ViewCam, 10/30/95.

Winners will be determined in random drawings conducted under the supervision of D.L. Blair, Inc., an independent judging organization whose decisions are final, from among all eligible entries received for that drawing. Approximate prize values are as follows: Panasonic wide-screen TV ($1,800); Wedgwood china ($840) and Sharp ViewCam ($2,000). Sweepstakes open to residents of the U.S. (except Puerto Rico) and Canada, 18 years of age or older. Employees and immediate family members of Harlequin Enterprises, Ltd., D.L. Blair, Inc., their affiliates, subsidiaries and all other agencies, entities and persons connected with the use, marketing or conduct of this sweepstakes are not eligible. Odds of winning a prize are dependent upon the number of eligible entries received for that drawing. Prize drawing and winner notification for each drawing will occur no later than 15 days after deadline for entry eligibility for that drawing. Limit: one prize to an individual, family or organization. All applicable laws and regulations apply. Sweepstakes offer void wherever prohibited by law. Any litigation within the province of Quebec respecting the conduct and awarding of the prizes in this sweepstakes must be submitted to the Regies des loteries et Courses du Quebec. In order to win a prize, residents of Canada will be required to correctly answer a time-limited arithmetical skill-testing question. Value of prizes are in U.S. currency.

Winners will be obligated to sign and return an Affidavit of Eligibility within 30 days of notification. In the event of noncompliance within this time period, prize may not be awarded. If any prize or prize notification is returned as undeliverable, that prize will not be awarded. By acceptance of a prize, winner consents to use of his/her name, photograph or other likeness for purposes of advertising, trade and promotion on behalf of Harlequin Enterprises, Ltd., without further compensation, unless prohibited by law.

For the names of prizewinners (available after 12/31/95), send a self-addressed, stamped envelope to: Prize Surprise Sweepstakes 3448 Winners, P.O. Box 4200, Blair, NE 68009.

RPZ KAL